Emma Thomson's

felicity Wishes

Big
Magical Mishaps

By *Emma Thomson and Helen Bailey*

Illustrated by *Emma Thomson*

How to make your felicity Wishes.

WISH

With this book comes an extra special wish for you and your best friend.

Hold the book together at each end and both close your eyes.

Wriggle your noses and think of a number under ten.

Open your eyes, whisper the numbers you thought of to each other.

Add these numbers together. This is your

Magic Number

you

best friend

Place your little finger on the stars, and say your magic number out loud together. Now make your wish quietly to yourselves. And maybe, one day, your wish might just come true.   Love

felicity

x

FELICITY WISHES®

Written by Emma Thomson and Helen Bailey

Illustrated by Emma Thomson

Felicity Wishes © 2000 Emma Thomson

Text © Emma Thomson and Helen Bailey

Illustrations © Emma Thomson

First published in Great Britain in 2002 for WHSmith

Greenbridge Road, Swindon, SN3 3LD

by Hodder Children's Books

This bind-up edition published 2004

A Catalogue record for this book is available from the British Library

ISBN 0 340 88223 9

The paper and board used in this paperback by Hodder Children's Books are natural recyclable products made from wood grown in sustainable forests. The manufacturing processes conform to the environmental regulations of the country of origin.

CONTENTS

Fashion Fiasco

Felicity Wishes was having a lovely, lazy morning in the garden flicking through the latest copy of *Fairy Girl* magazine. There were lots of really pretty dresses and loads of interesting articles, but the one that had caught her eye was called: 'A Brand New Outfit Equals A Brand New You!' There was a picture of pop star Suzi Sparkle wearing all sorts of dresses, though most of them seemed to be black and none of them had the full skirts Felicity loved so much. Felicity quite liked the *old* her, but a new one sounded interesting. And it was the perfect excuse to go shopping!

"I think," she said to herself out loud as she skipped out of the front door, "that if I'm going to buy a new outfit for a new me, I'll have to go to some new shops!"

So, instead of turning right when she left her house to go down Feather Hill to the shops in Little Blossoming, she turned left and headed up the hill towards Bloomfield. The shops there were well-known for stocking the latest clothes from the hottest fairy fashion designers. Felicity couldn't wait to start trying on the trendiest things!

* * *

First stop was Miss Fairy, described in Felicity's magazine as 'the top shopping experience for the fashion-conscious fairy'.

And there, in the window, was one of the dresses Suzi Sparkle had been wearing in *Fairy Girl*!

Excitedly, Felicity pushed the door open and popped inside.

Miss Fairy

But, instead of the row upon row of brightly-coloured dresses she'd expected to find, just a few dark-coloured dresses hung in the shadows on matt black rails. Everything was neat, clean and perfect. Felicity felt she was messing up the shop just by being there!

It all seemed quite cold and unfriendly, even down to the fairy assistant who was now heading towards Felicity. She was dressed from head to toe in black, including black wings and a black crown. Even her hair, which was pulled back from her head in a high ponytail, was black. Felicity thought she looked like a giant crow.

"Can I help you?" said the assistant, in a voice which made Felicity think the *last* thing she wanted to do was help.

Shyly, Felicity smoothed down the folds in her skirt, looked up and said as bravely as she could, "I like the dress in the window, but do you have it in pink?"

The assistant looked as if she had swallowed a huge toffee apple in one go.

"We're not stocking *any* pink this year," she said dramatically. "This year, black is the new pink."

Felicity really wanted pink - lilac at a pinch. What was the point of treating yourself to a special outfit if you couldn't buy it in the colour you wanted?

"Don't you have *any* colour other than black?" Felicity asked the crow.

"If madam feels uncomfortable

going straight to black we have other shades such as dark grey, charcoal, midnight black and stormy sky."

"No pink?" asked Felicity.

"No pink," said the assistant firmly. Seeing Felicity's disappointed face, the assistant offered to phone one of their branches to see if they had any pink dresses.

"Tamara? It's Flora from Miss Fairy in Bloomfield. We have a customer here who wants style number 1422 in — " she almost spat out the word, "–PINK!"

Felicity could hear Tamara sniggering down the phone while Flora whispered to her. Felicity thought they were both very rude. Then she remembered the pictures of Suzi Sparkle wearing the black dresses in *Fairy Girl*. Perhaps it *was* time to try something different. She grabbed the dress off the rail, checked the size and said to the assistant (who was still giggling and whispering into the phone), "I'll take this one!"

* * *

Felicity didn't feel as skippy and bubbly as she normally did after buying a dress. In fact, she felt rather flat. It wasn't quite the dress she wanted and it *certainly* wasn't the colour she'd dreamed of. Still, at least she would be at the height of fashion!

She could always dress it up with some sparkly new accessories.

So her next stop was Trinkets, which sold every sort of fairy accessory you could imagine.

The shop assistant in Trinkets was much more friendly than the snooty Flora. When she asked whether she could help Felicity, she seemed to really mean it.

"I'd like a new wand, please," said Felicity.

The shop assistant had spied her shopping bag.

"Ah," she said, "I see you have been to Miss Fairy. You are obviously a very fashion-conscious young fairy."

Felicity was thrilled. That was *exactly* what she was! A fairy with her wand on the pulse of fairy fashion!

"Can I suggest this year's latest look in wands?" said the assistant.

She brought out a terribly thin

and fragile-looking black stick with a blob on the end.

Both Felicity and the assistant stared at it intently.

Finally Felicity asked, "Does it work?"

The assistant looked embarrassed and coughed.

"It's fair to say that some of my customers have found its waving powers to be…

umm…

limited."

She leaned closer to Felicity and wrinkled her nose. "Between you and me, I'd only carry it on occasions when you know you're not going to need it."

Felicity wondered how she would know in advance whether she needed it or not. She was only a young fairy and hadn't yet left fairy school, but even though she hadn't been granted her own full fairy powers, the wand still looked ridiculously weedy. It was fashionable though, and that was the most important thing.

Next, the shop assistant suggested a new crown to go with the wand, equally small but, Felicity reminded herself, terribly fashionable!

With a new dress, a new wand and a new crown, she might as well go the whole way and get some new wings. As a young fairy she wasn't allowed to have a full pair of wings

with a double flutter, but she could
choose any pair of single flutter
wings she set her heart on.

In Wings 'N' Things she showed
the shop assistant her little Fairy
Identity Card and was sent over to
the 'Beginner Fairy' wings section.

Felicity thought there had been
a mistake as the wings were so tiny.
She was a beginner fairy, not a
baby one!

She went back to the assistant
and showed her ID card again.

"I am at fairy school," she stressed.
"I can have bigger wings."

The assistant was busy sticking
glitter 'go-faster' stripes on her shoes
and didn't look up, but said, "All the
manufacturers have shrunk their
wings this year. Micro wings are the
'in' thing. We can hardly keep up
with demand."

Felicity couldn't remember any of

her friends wearing such teeny tiny wings, and there was something suspicious about the racks and racks of them on display, despite the shop assistant telling her they kept selling out.

She took a pair of the wings off the rack and looked at the swing ticket. "All the power of a standard wing in a simple, stylish design," it read. "For the modern fairy on the move!"

"A modern fairy on the move," she repeated to herself. "That's me! These wings will be just right!"

Now all that was left to buy was a new pair of tights.

By this time, Felicity knew better than to ask for pink stripy tights. She *was* a modern fashion-conscious fairy on the move after all!

Proudly swinging her bags, she asked for something she never thought she'd have wanted in a million fairy years. She asked for a pair of black-and-white stripy tights. The assistant gave her a knowing smile and swiftly brought her a pair. "She must recognise me as someone who knows all about fashion," Felicity thought.

Felicity was really exhausted when she got home with all her new things. Some of her purchases may have been small but they still seemed heavy. She

decided to have a big mug of hot
chocolate with extra whipped cream
and sugar to give her an energy
boost. Then she would try on her new
outfit and see what the new Felicity
Wishes looked like.

✳ ✳ ✳

Feeling better after her hot
chocolate, Felicity began to unwrap
her goodies. First came the dress
from Miss Fairy, as worn in *Fairy Girl*
by pop star Suzi Sparkle. The dress
was very long and very black. Felicity

looked at the picture of Suzi and then back at her reflection in the mirror.

Suzi looked beautiful, elegant and chic draped across a sofa wearing the dress.

Felicity just looked – and felt – very uncomfortable. She could hardly bend down to put on her new tights. When she did get them on, what a shock! The tights were indeed black-and-white as she had asked, but the stripes weren't going across, they were going lengthways! Felicity thought she looked more like a giant mint humbug than the elegant Suzi Sparkle.

Things were *not* going according to plan. The micro wings were so tiny they kept popping out of her hands. After a great deal of twisting and turning she finally got them on. Time to try them out!

Felicity flew up to the ceiling.

Because the wings were so small they had to flutter twice as fast as her usual wings to achieve the same height. There was the most awful buzzing noise as if a fly was stuck in the lamp.

Felicity looked around. She couldn't see a fly, but the noise continued. Then she realised it was coming from her wings! They were fluttering so fast they were buzzing. Her super new micro fashion wings were making the noise of a monster bee!

* * *

Back on the ground, Felicity unwrapped the thin wand which wouldn't wave, and tried on the crown, which was so tiny it kept slipping off her head.

She looked at herself in the mirror again.

She had a dress she couldn't move in.

A pair of wings she couldn't fly in.

A wand she couldn't wave.

A crown that wouldn't stay on.

And a pair of tights which were just... horrible.

The doorbell chimed.

Felicity found she couldn't even walk to the door. Her dress was so long and narrow she had to jump up and down as if she was on a pogo stick. It took such a time for Felicity to get to the door, the bell rang again.

When she opened the door, Polly, Holly and Daisy stared at their friend for a moment before collapsing with laughter.

"What ARE you wearing?" asked Polly, her eyes streaming with tears of laughter.

"Are you off to a fancy dress party?" enquired Holly between fits of giggles.

So Felicity explained about seeing Suzi Sparkle in *Fairy Girl* and how she wanted to be a fashionable fairy on the move, but now she was a fashionable fairy who couldn't move and she really didn't like the new Felicity as much as the old one.

"What has Suzi Sparkle got that I haven't?" asked Felicity who was now laughing as much as her friends.

Holly, who had been reading the article while Felicity told her tale of shopping woe, pointed at the picture of the reclining Suzi.

"No wonder she's draped across a sofa," she said. "She probably can't stand up!"

"She probably *was* standing up but

tripped and landed on the sofa and is now stranded!" shrieked Polly.

When Felicity demonstrated the micro wings with their high-pitched buzz they begged her to stop. They were laughing so much their tummies ached!

Daisy came over to Felicity and put her arms around her. She hugged her so tightly, Felicity's tiny crown popped off.

"Felicity," she said, "we love you just the way you are. We don't *want* a new Felicity, we like the old one!"

"I don't think Suzi Sparkle would be as good fun as you, or such a good friend," added Polly. "It's what's on the inside that counts, not on the outside!"

"What am I going to do with all these things?" said Felicity, looking down at her humbug legs.

"We'll take them back tomorrow," said Daisy. "I'm sure there won't be a problem. In the meantime, you have five minutes to get out of all that black and into something pink and then we'll all go out for an ice-cream!"

it doesn't matter
what's on the
outside

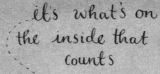

it's what's on
the inside that
counts

Decorating Disaster

Felicity Wishes and her friends were lolling about on Felicity's bed, planning what they were going to do during the half-term break from the School of Nine Wishes. They had one week - just long enough to have masses of fun!

"So," said Polly. "What's it to be? Shopping, shopping or more shopping?"

"I think," said Felicity, looking around her bedroom, "I'm going to re-decorate."

"Does it really need it?" asked Holly, flipping through a magazine without looking up. Decorating was not Holly's idea of fun at all. In fact, anything that required hard work sounded like a very bad idea indeed.

"*Need* doesn't come into it," said Felicity firmly. "I feel like a change."

"It does seem a shame to take down this lovely wallpaper," said Daisy. "It looks almost new to me."

Polly peered up at the ceiling. "I can see a bit of paper peeling - right there, in the corner."

"You see!" exclaimed Felicity triumphantly. "The room does need a make-over!"

"Just stick some glue on it!" said Holly, now becoming worried. "Glue it, let's go shopping and we'll think about decorating later!"

Felicity found some Soopa Doopa glue and Polly flew up to the ceiling to inspect the damage. In one corner there was a tiny piece of wallpaper which had come away from the wall.

"What's it to be, Felicity?" Polly shouted down. "Are we decorating or not?"

Felicity suddenly thought of all the work that needed to be done before the fun could start: moving furniture, taking down posters, removing the curtains, covering up the carpet, cleaning the walls. Even though her friends would help her, perhaps they *should* wait for the long summer holidays.

"Glue it!" shouted Felicity. "We'll leave the decorating for another time."

Holly let out a great sigh of relief and went back to reading magazines.

Polly squeezed a little Soopa Doopa glue out of the tube, but it wouldn't stop. The glue kept on spilling out of the tube in a huge sticky mess. On and on it oozed.

"The glue is going wild! I can't stop it coming out of the tube," she yelled down to her friends.

"Put some on the wallpaper, Pol!" shouted Felicity

"Put the cap back on!" shrieked Daisy.

Holly could feel a headache coming on.

* * *

The glue was getting everywhere. Everything Polly touched seemed to become covered with a layer of super sticky goo.

"I'm flying back down!" called Polly. "There's enough glue up here to stick glitter to every fairy wand in Little Blossoming!"

But as Polly flew down, there was the most tremendous ripping sound.

In amongst the sticky mess, a corner
of Polly's right wing had become
stuck to the wall. Streaming behind
her like a huge paper cape was
Felicity's wallpaper!

"Arghh…" shrieked Polly as she
landed with a thump on the carpet,
the wallpaper floating down and
covering her in a huge gooey blanket.

"That's torn it!" said Holly, as the
fairies rushed over
to their crumpled
friend.

With a large strip of wallpaper now covering Polly rather than the wall, there was nothing for it but to redecorate the room after all.

Everyone was already in such a mess that Daisy, Polly and Felicity decided to strip the rest of the wallpaper off the walls there and then, while Holly covered up the furniture with some large white sheets. They used the stars on their wands to prise away bits of wallpaper, then flew about the room pulling off strips like fat paper streamers.

When they had finished, they bundled all the mess into the bin, cleaned themselves up, had a cup of hot chocolate and set off for Do-It-Together to find something special to decorate Felicity's room with.

* * *

The shop was bustling with fairies buying paint and paper of every pattern and colour imaginable.

There was wallpaper with stripes going up and stripes going across. Wallpaper with big checks you could play noughts and crosses on, and wallpaper with checks so tiny they made your eyes go funny. There was paper with glow-in-the dark stars so you could imagine you were sleeping outside, and paper with sparkles that would wake you up in the morning with a twinkle when the sun shone through the curtains. There was so much to choose from!

Then Felicity saw a design she loved.

It was pale pink with enormous deep pink roses the size of dinner plates. Felicity thought it was gorgeous. The others weren't so sure.

"Don't you think the roses are a bit – well – *large*?" said Daisy, looking doubtfully at the design.

"They're humungous!" said Polly. "Far too large for your bedroom, Felicity. How about something more delicate?"

But Felicity was already hugging rolls of the paper. There was no dissuading her.

So the others gathered together some brushes, a bucket, some wallpaper paste and a hard hat for Holly (who was worried about her hair), then set off back to Felicity's house.

The first problem was finding a table long enough for the wallpaper. Holly suggested they used the ironing board which wasn't perfect but, if Daisy held the end of the paper carefully, might just work.

Polly opened the packet of wallpaper paste and sneezed so hard she added too much powder to the bucket of morning dew, making the paste as lumpy as porridge. Even her frantic whisking with the end of her wand didn't appear to make any difference.

Holly cut the wallpaper into a long strip, then put it on the ironing board. Felicity brushed the lumpy paste on to the back of the paper. With so much paste the wallpaper was very heavy and Daisy, Polly and Felicity had trouble lifting it up and flying to the ceiling to hang it.

Holly didn't like heights so she

shouted out instructions
from below.

"Up a bit, left a bit, right
a bit – hang!"

They fluttered up and
down smoothing out the
lumps, then stood back
to admire their handiwork.

The roses were, indeed,
humungous. Daisy had
been right, they were far
too big for Felicity's cosy
bedroom. But, more
worryingly, right in the
centre of the paper was
a huge bulge.

The friends looked at each
other, puzzled.

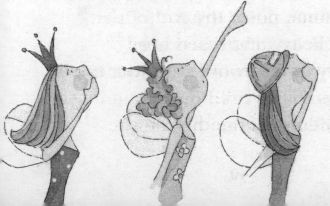

"What is that lump?" asked Holly.

"We smoothed the top, didn't we?" said Daisy to Felicity.

"And Polly and I did the bottom…" said Holly.

But no one had done the middle!

The fairies inspected the lump. It was large, and hard and brush-shaped.

"We've papered over the paste brush!" giggled Felicity.

The friends fell about laughing. Time to start again! But Felicity had had enough of the wallpaper with its huge roses and strange bulges.

"We've only done one sheet, it's been a disaster and I don't like the pattern after all. Let's take it back and get some paint instead."

"But Felicity," chorused her friends, "you've always said you think plain walls are boring!"

"A fairy can change her mind,

can't she?" Felicity replied, gathering up the unused rolls of rose-patterned paper before setting off to Do-It-Together again.

There was an even wider choice of paint colours than there had been of wallpaper patterns, but the fairies knew exactly which colour Felicity would choose. Pink. The question was, which shade?

There was a lovely dusty pink the same colour as Daisy's roses, a fabulous deep pink which Felicity knew would match her duvet beautifully, a delicate light pink that shimmered and was very special, and a pink that reminded Felicity of strawberry ice-cream.

"Oh, they're all yummy! I just don't know which one to choose," said Felicity, as she lined up the tins of paint. She closed her eyes and began, "I spy, with my closed eye..."

Daisy was horrified. "Felicity! You can't choose a colour like that!"

"It's the best way," said Felicity. "There's no such thing as a horrible pink, so whichever one I choose will be perfect."

She shut her eyes and began again, pointing randomly at the tins.

"I spy, with my closed eye, a colour beginning with P!" Felicity's finger stopped on a beautiful pinky lilac colour called 'Twilight Blush'.

It was perfect.

They each got a paint brush, a furry roller, and a pot of white paint for the skirting boards and, for the second time that day, headed back to Felicity's house to start decorating.

Painting was much more fun than papering and the fairies quickly covered the walls with a generous coat of 'Twilight Blush'. They also covered themselves with a layer of paint. The tin said "non-drip" but it didn't say "non-splash" and soon they all looked as if they had a bad case of chicken pox!

After Holly had painted the skirting boards white, they declared the room finished. It looked lovely.

"It's gorgeous, Felicity," said Polly.

"Your method of choosing a colour worked brilliantly after all," agreed Daisy.

Felicity was very quiet.

"Don't you like your new room?" asked Holly wearily. "*Please* tell me that you like it."

"I do," mumbled Felicity, looking down at her toes. What was a little white lie to save her friends' feelings?

But her friends knew her too well and her face said it all. Polly raised one eyebrow in an "are you sure?" kind of way.

"Honestly... I... er... do," said Felicity hesitantly. "It's just after wallpaper, the plain walls look a little... well... *plain*."

This time it was the turn of her friends to remain silent. They stared at her with their paint-splashed faces.

"I mean," said Felicity sensing her friends' despair and beginning to gabble, "I love the colour, but it's just a little... um... *boring*. It needs a pattern."

The fairies groaned. Holly threw herself on to the sheet-covered bed.

"It's at times like this that I'd really love to have graduated from the School of Nine Wishes," she moaned. "If I was a fully-qualified fairy I could just wave my magic wand and instantly transform your room to look however you wanted it. You could change your mind a hundred times and it wouldn't matter."

"Don't you think that might be thought of as a waste of a wish?" said Polly. One of the first lessons they had ever had at fairy school was the importance of using your wishes wisely. Polly wasn't sure that providing Felicity with the right wallpaper and paint counted as a wise wish.

Holly thought for a moment. "The fairy motto starts off saying: I promise to take good care of my

wishes. To use them wisely for the
good of others. We would be using
a wish to help Felicity."

"Are you sure that would be your
only reason, though? To help Felicity?"
asked Polly, looking worried. "Don't
forget, the motto goes on to say:
Never to use them for my own gain.
And to try my best to live by the Fairy
Motto. By changing Felicity's room it
means less work for us. Surely that's

using a wish for our own gain?"

Daisy suddenly had an idea. "I know! We can still use our magic wands to transform Felicity's room, but without making a wish. Holly, have you got any white paint left?"

Holly handed over the tin to Daisy, who carefully dipped the end of the handle of her wand into the paint and dabbed it on to the pink wall. It made a perfect white spot. She then dipped one of the points of the star

in the paint and made eight tiny
spots around the first larger spot.
She stood back to let Polly, Holly
and Felicity see. She had painted
a small, white, perfectly formed
flower.

"Daisy!" exclaimed Felicity hugging
her friend. "That's brilliant! You are
so clever."

Daisy turned a sort of 'Twilight
Blush' colour and said, "Let's use
our wands to cover all the walls."

So the four friends spent the rest
of the day dipping and dabbing,
painting flowers on the walls with
their wands. When they finally
finished and the last flower had
been painted, Felicity couldn't have
been happier. Not only did she have
a beautiful pink bedroom, but one
where each flower had been hand-
painted with care by the friends she
loved most. Every single flower would

always remind her how lucky she
was to have such good
fairy friends!

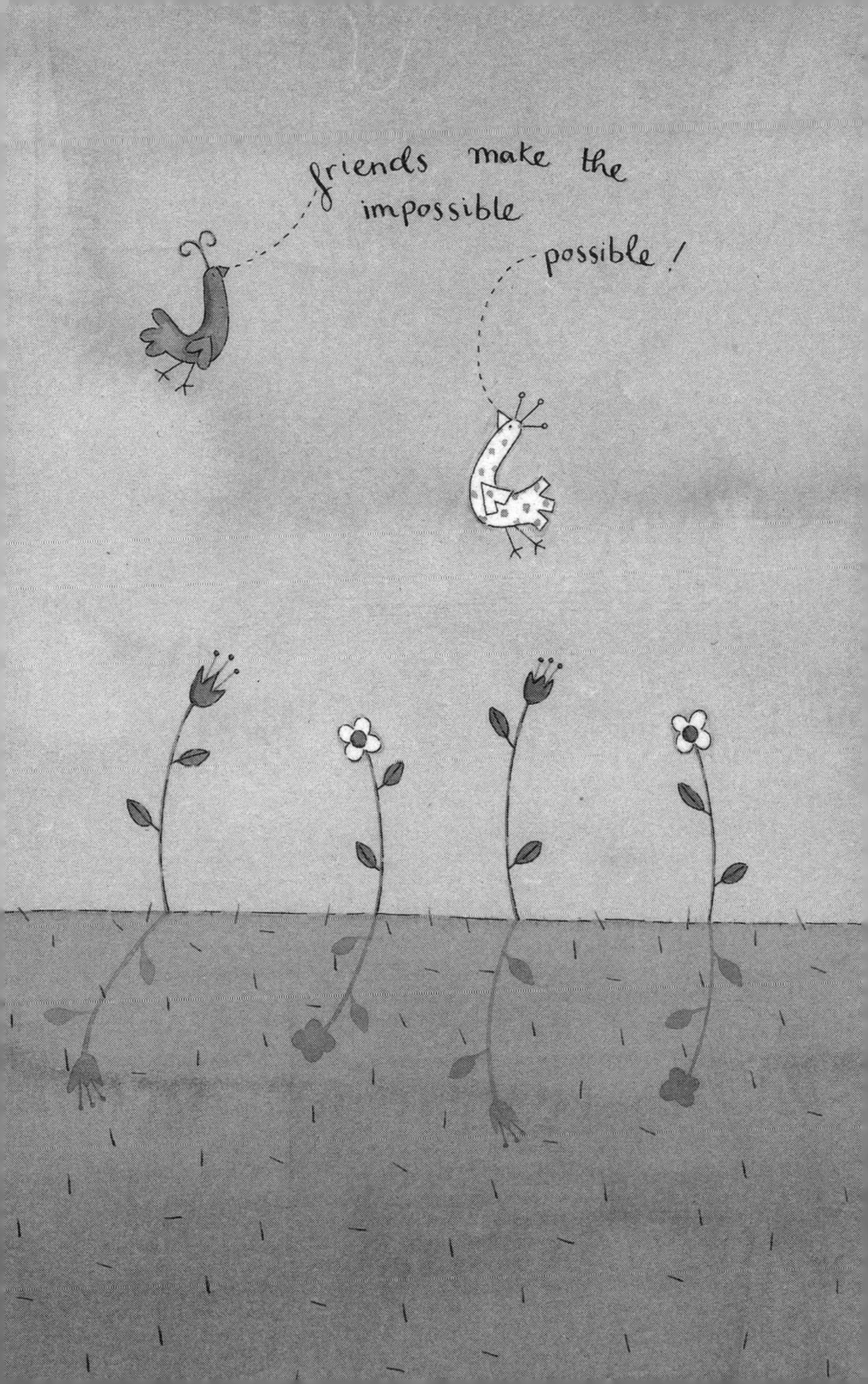
friends make the impossible
possible!

Skating Surprise

The doorbell chimed several times before Felicity managed to get to the door.

"I'm coming! I'm coming!" she called out. Someone was in a great rush to see her. When she finally opened her door, Daisy and Polly were standing on the doorstep. They were flushed with excitement and were carrying their ice-skates over their shoulders.

"Felicity! Quickly! Find your skates," said Daisy breathlessly.

"The ice rink has opened for the first time this winter. The queue will be enormous once word gets round."

Polly was equally excited. "If we're quick we can spend the whole afternoon skating," she said. "Holly is meeting us there in twenty minutes."

Skating! Felicity loved skating. She couldn't wait to get on the ice.

"Come in while I find my skates," she said to her friends, who obviously didn't want to waste even a minute of precious skating time.

Felicity started looking for her skates in the hall cupboard, while Daisy chattered on about how lucky it was that she had been to the library to return her book on tropical plants. It hadn't been due back for another few days, but she'd found it so interesting she'd finished it already.

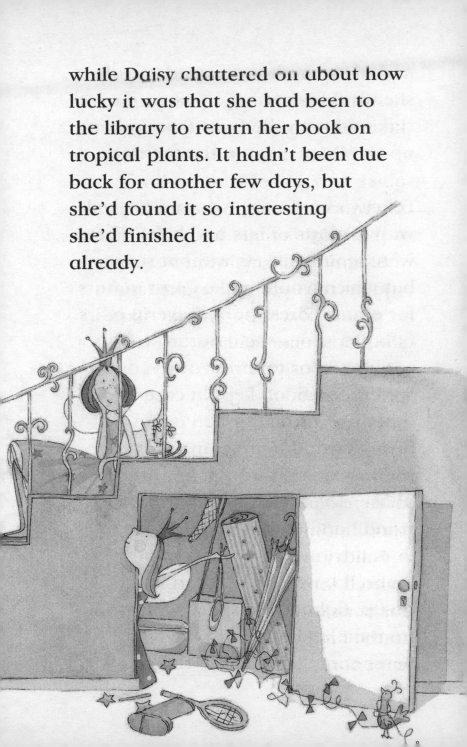

And, if she hadn't returned it early, she would never have passed the ice rink and seen the Frost Fairy putting up an 'Open' sign at the entrance...

* * *

Felicity's cupboard was jam-packed with all sorts of bits and bobs. There were tennis rackets without strings, but which would make great guitars for a fancy dress party; several pairs of ballet shoes she'd outgrown but couldn't bear to throw away; one Wellington boot, kept in case the other one turned up; an awful orange wand handle, from when she was going through her orange phase; several stars that had no wand handles, but might come in handy one day; and a large umbrella, which would no longer go up, fighting for space with string from the end of a kite which had never come down. Everything, in fact, except a pair of ice-skates.

"I know I've seen them somewhere," she said to her friends, who were hopping up and down trying to conceal their impatience. The question was, where?

"They're probably with your missing welly," said Polly unhelpfully.

Felicity looked in every cupboard she could think of and pulled out every drawer she had. She looked under the bed and found several pairs of tights she thought she'd lost.

She flew up to look on top of the wardrobe and discovered her secret diary, which she'd put in a place so secret even she hadn't been able to find it for weeks.

Behind the sofa she found her half-finished project on Famous Fairies in History, while an inspection of the kitchen cupboard revealed a fairy cake so old it was almost fossilized.

But there was no sign of the skates. Not even a broken lace!

There was nowhere else to look.

"Don't worry," said Daisy, who didn't want to wait any longer. "You can borrow some at the rink."

✳ ✳ ✳

The rink was already busy when they arrived. Fairies were rushing around, trying on skates, tightening up laces and making their way to the glistening ice. One fairy was already on the ice speed-skating, turning sharply, spraying tiny ice crystals everywhere.

"Show off," thought Holly, as she waved at her friends. They made their way over to her. Holly was surprised to see that Felicity didn't

have any skates, and raised an
eyebrow at her.

"I don't know where my skates
have got to," explained Felicity. "I'm
just off to borrow some."

It had taken them so long to look
for Felicity's skates, the ice rink was
now packed. By the time they got to
the front of the queue, most of the
skates had already
been borrowed.

"What size are you?" asked the
fairy behind the desk.

"An eighth of a standard wand," said Felicity, peering over the attendant's shoulder at the rows of nearly empty shelves.

"You're out of luck," said the fairy. "The nearest size is a tenth of a compact wand, but that of course comes in a much narrower fitting. It will be far too small for you."

Felicity was determined to skate with her friends.

"It'll be fine," she said confidently.

But it was far from fine. The boots were so small she could hardly get her feet into them, even when she reluctantly took off her tights. When she finally got both feet into the boots, she could barely move. Her toes were crinkled up at the end and the laces were too short for her to do them up. And, without her warm tights, her legs began to get hundreds of little goosebumps and turn quite blue. Even Felicity had to admit defeat.

She took them back to the attendant, who eyed her with an "I told you so" sort of expression.

"As you don't have my size, I think it would be better to have boots that are too big rather than too small. I can always wear extra socks!" she said to the attendant, who handed her what seemed like the longest pair of skating boots she had ever seen and a huge bundle of old socks.

Felicity put on all four pairs of socks (today wasn't a day to be worried about how she looked), but still the boots were far too big. Carefully, she made her way

to the ice. Holly, Daisy and Polly had
joined the end of a long line of
fairies skating around the rink. Daisy
held out her hand and Felicity
grasped it to join the line.

At first everything went well.
The line snaked around the rink
slowly and although Felicity could
hardly lift her feet, let alone point
them in the right direction, all she
had to do was hang on to Daisy. As
the fairies got more confident on the
ice, though, the faster they skated.
Giggling and squealing with delight,

they cut through the crisp ice faster
and faster.

By now, all Felicity could do was
hang on and hope for the best. Her
boots were so heavy and her feet
so long she had no idea in which
direction they were pointing.

Finally, it all got too much. The
line headed towards a corner at top
speed but Felicity couldn't
turn her feet.
The
corner
got
nearer
and nearer
and the line of
skaters got
faster and
faster,

but Felicity's feet felt like long blocks of concrete. As the corner loomed up she shouted, "I've lost control of my feet!" so loudly that Daisy dropped her hand in surprise, and Felicity zoomed straight ahead at such a speed that she shot through the gap in the barrier, across the carpet and landed on a chair in the coffee shop.

The other fairies hurried off the ice to see whether she was all right.

Felicity was fine, just a little embarrassed.

So they sat and drank mugs of steaming hot chocolate and whipped cream, and stared at the size of Felicity's boots. They'd never seen a pair so big and couldn't imagine what sort of a fairy would wear them. Whatever sort of fairy it was, it certainly wasn't Felicity! The boots would have to go back.

"It's such a shame none of us have your size feet," said Holly, "or we could take it in turns to lend you our boots."

Felicity had what she thought was a brilliant idea.

"I could fly above you when you skate so at least I'm not missing out completely. We can still have fun together."

✻ ✻ ✻

But Felicity's brilliant idea was
not so brilliant in practice.

Daisy, Holly
and Polly
set off on the
ice and Felicity
flew just above them.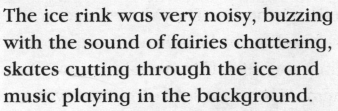
The ice rink was very noisy, buzzing
with the sound of fairies chattering,
skates cutting through the ice and
music playing in the background.

Felicity flew around the rink a few
times following her friends but it
was too noisy to hear what they
were saying. They were chattering
and giggling and waving to Felicity.
Felicity waved back but really she
wanted to hear what her friends
were talking about. They seemed to
be having such fun!

As Felicity couldn't quite hear
what the others were saying, she
flew a little lower. She still couldn't

hear, so she flew lower still. So low in
fact, that her skirt covered Daisy's head.
Poor Daisy couldn't see *anything*.
Soon she sent the rest of her
friends sprawling
over the ice.

"Let's all go home," said Polly, dusting the ice off her dress and helping Daisy smooth her crumpled wings. "We can come back another day when Felicity has found her skates."

"I'm so sorry," said Felicity. "I wish I could magic some skates that were the right size."

"Felicity!" exclaimed Polly, slightly shocked. "You know you're not allowed to make wishes for yourself!"

"I don't think saying 'I wish I could' counts," said Holly, who felt rules were made to be broken.

"It might," said Polly who felt rules were there for a good reason, even if you didn't always know what that reason was.

They had only just started practising simple wishes at The School of Nine Wishes, and then only under the supervision of the Fairy

Godmother. Even so, there had been some disasters. While practising a wish to stop ice cream from melting, Felicity's ice cream became so frozen that her lips stuck to it when she tried to lick it.

Fairy Godmother had to perform a wish to melt it instantly, which unstuck the ice cream cone, but sent melted ice cream all over Felicity's dress. Everyone but Fairy Godmother thought it was very funny, though

Felicity's lips felt sore for days afterwards.

Felicity was determined her forgetfulness wasn't going to spoil her friends' fun.

"You stay here and I'll go home," she said firmly. "Come back to my house afterwards and we'll toast crumpets."

Felicity unlaced the boots, took out her feet and removed the four pairs of socks. Without her boots, her feet felt as light as whipped cream, though her heart felt a little heavy leaving her friends behind. She could see them sweeping across the ice again, laughing and having fun. A new line of fairies had been formed and they were holding each other around the waist, snaking round the rink.

Still, she reminded herself, as Daisy had said, there would be other days.

* * *

As she was leaving the ice rink, Felicity saw Floella. Floella had already graduated from The School of Nine Wishes and was now a Frost Fairy, responsible for turning winter into spring and autumn into winter. As Floella was older and already a proper fairy with full magic powers, Felicity didn't think Floella would notice her. She wouldn't get simple wishes wrong and certainly not ones involving ice cream!

But Floella *had* seen Felicity and she stopped to talk.

"It's Felicity Wishes, isn't it?" she said. "Are you leaving already?"

Felicity was amazed that Floella had even paused to talk to her, but even *more* surprised that she knew her name. She started to tell Floella about the lost skates, how she thought she might have broken two of the most important fairy rules –

not to use wishes for your own good
and certainly not to use them before
you were qualified to do so – and
about the incident at school when
her tongue got stuck
to the ice cream.

Floella smiled at Felicity kindly.
"All young fairies make mistakes

when they first start at fairy school - and even when they leave. I know I do! Don't worry about being perfect. Just always try to do your best at everything you do!"

Felicity couldn't believe that Floella did anything other than make perfect wishes every time, but it was nice to know even she had off days!

"I bet you don't lose your skates, though," said Felicity.

Floella laughed and looked down at her own gleaming pair.

"Well no, a frost fairy without skates would be a disaster! In fact, I carry a spare pair with me in case of emergencies. Would you like to borrow them? They're an eighth of a standard wand. Do you think they might fit you?"

"I can't believe it – they're exactly my size. Can I really borrow them?"

Felicity was jumping up and down
with joy.

Floella handed her the skates.
"Don't forget to let me have them
back!" she said.

As Felicity was thanking Floella,
she suddenly remembered where
her old skates were!

"I let a young fairy borrow them
last year just as I was leaving the
ice rink and she must have forgotten
to give them back to me!"

Felicity was just about to hurry to
join her friends when Floella called
out her name. Felicity turned back.

"I'm not recommending you
make wishes yet," said Floella, "but
sometimes, if it's done with the right
intentions, it does no harm." And
with that Floella flew off - leaving

Felicity wondering whether she really *had* made a wish for skates, or whether bumping into Floella had just been a happy accident...

Swimming Secrets

The weather in Little Blossoming was glorious. Felicity and her friends were sitting in the sunshine on the front step of Polly's house, warming their wings in the early summer sun.

"Ooh, this is lovely," said Felicity, stretching out her legs and letting one of her shoes drop off. "Summer is *definitely* on its way!"

"The weather forecast said that summer would be here by the weekend," said Daisy. "It's going to get hotter and hotter. I must make sure my plants have enough water."

Felicity had an idea.

"If it's going to be really hot on Saturday, why don't we fly to Glitter Beach? It's always a bit cooler by the sea."

"Ooh yes!" exclaimed the fairies together. All except Polly.

Daisy noticed Polly looking worried.

"What's wrong, Pol?" she asked. "Don't you fancy splashing in the sea and wriggling your toes in the sand?"

Polly looked down at her feet and bit her lip. "Umm... er... I've got some homework to finish," she said.

The fairies looked at her in panic. Was there some homework they'd

forgotten about? Polly was *always*
the first to hand her homework in,
whereas Felicity put off today
anything she could do tomorrow.

"I thought I'd handed everything
in!" said Daisy.

"Oh no!" groaned Holly, putting
her head in her hands. "Not more
work!"

"What homework haven't you
finished?" asked Felicity.

Polly was still looking
uncomfortable, and
said vaguely, "Well,
not homework
exactly. I'm
writing a story
called *Toothy Tales*, just for fun."

Everyone knew Polly wanted to
be a Tooth Fairy. She was the kind
of fairy who was good at *everything*
she tried. Polly had come top in
history for remembering all the

famous fairies' names. In chemistry
her sparkle dust had a twinkle no
other dust could match. And in
geography she could find countries
on the globe with her eyes closed.
But her real passion was smiles.
Toothy smiles, gappy
smiles, wide smiles,
tiny smiles, *any*
smiles!

"Thank goodness for that!"
exclaimed Felicity, relieved that her
day at the beach wouldn't be spoilt
by the thought of homework still to
do. "If it's for fun, then it won't have
a date to be handed in by – so you
can come to the beach after all!"

Polly still didn't look happy.

"It's quite a long flight to the beach and if it's hot we'll be really tired by the time we get there," she protested.

Daisy couldn't see a problem.

"I'm going to need to be up early to water all the plants," she said. "Let's *all* get up early and fly to the beach before it gets really hot."

"But we'll still have the journey back!" said Polly desperately.

This just wasn't like Polly at all, thought her friends. Polly was sensible, but she was always keen to do fun things. If they went cycling, the others would be pedalling off while Polly was still checking that her chain was fixed properly. Polly never started a recipe without checking she had all the ingredients first, whereas Felicity would get halfway through a recipe for chocolate cake before finding out she had no chocolate. And, even though Polly was brilliant at geography, she would look at the map *before* she set off, rather than wait until she got lost.

"Polly," said Felicity, putting her arm around her friend, "remember what a glorious day we had at the beach last year? We swam in the bay and ate oodles of pink sugary candy floss and..."

Felicity suddenly stopped. "I don't remember you coming last year, actually - but I can't remember why."

"You weren't feeling well," said Holly.

"That's final, then!" said Daisy. "You can't go another year without going to Glitter Beach! Forget your story. Don't worry about how long it will take to get there. Let's meet really early tomorrow morning and head for sun, sea and candy floss!"

Daisy had a big sun umbrella which she and Holly could carry between them. Felicity said she would make a picnic. Everyone was to bring their own towels, and Holly promised enough sun cream to share. Last year she had got rather burnt and was nicknamed Holly Berry for the rest of the summer!

Holly was going to stay the night at Felicity's house, so Daisy promised to knock on their door in the morning, on the way to pick up Polly. The plan was made!

Polly couldn't sleep that night. The room was hot and she tossed and turned.

One o'clock.

Two o'clock.

Not even her favourite
pillow felt comfortable.

Just as she thought
she was drifting
off to sleep,
Polly woke
up with a
start.

Her heart was racing so fast she
could hear it beating.

She got up and went to the window.
The sky was full of tiny silver stars
and the moon seemed to be smiling
down at her.

"Oh Moon," she sighed. "How am
I going to tell my friends about my
terrible secret?"

* * *

Polly finally managed to fall asleep not long before she was due to get up.

In fact, she was still snuggled so deep under the covers when her friends arrived she didn't hear them ringing the front door bell.

Daisy flew up to Polly's bedroom window and tapped on the glass.

Still half-asleep, Polly tugged herself out of bed, rubbed her eyes and slowly went downstairs to open the front door.

When she saw the big beach umbrella, her tummy did a somersault. Today was the day!

"I don't feel well," she said in a feeble voice to her friends. "You have a lovely time at the beach. I think I'll just stay here at home."

"You're just sleepy. We felt horrible having to get up so early but we feel super now, don't we, Holly?" said Felicity, nudging Holly, who was

leaning against the
doorframe yawning,
her eyes half-shut.

Polly trudged back
up the stairs to get
dressed. Opening her
cupboard she saw
her purple, spotty
swimming costume
folded neatly on
one of the shelves.

Perhaps there was one last chance!

Grabbing the costume from the
cupboard, she shouted downstairs
to her friends, "There's a problem!
I can't find my swimsuit. Go on
without me!"

But before Polly had a chance to
hide her costume under the mattress,
Felicity had flown up the stairs and
was standing in her bedroom.

Felicity was always amazed at how
neat Polly's room was. All her wings

were freshly ironed and
hung neatly in the wardrobe.
Her jars of sparkle-dust were each
sealed with a tiny label and arranged
in order of strength. Her school wand
was lying on top of her school bag,
which was packed and ready for
Monday morning and, even though
Polly had only just got out of it, her
bed looked barely crumpled.

"You *are* sleepy!" laughed Felicity,
pointing at the purple swimsuit.
"Look! You're holding it!"

* * *

Little Blossoming glittered in the early
morning sun. As they flew over
the rooftops, the fairies could
see the town just beginning
to wake up below them.
Outside Sparkles,
their favourite café, a
fairy was putting out
tables and chairs.

Another fairy was delivering copies of the *Daily Flutter*, trying to push the newspapers through tiny letterboxes. Someone else was cycling slowly up Feather Hill, while two fairies jogged down it.

The friends flew over The School of Nine Wishes, with its golden gates, and across Nine Wish Wood, which belonged to the school.

Daisy could see her garden now, which was packed so full of flowers it looked like a huge burst of colour beneath them.

As they left Little Blossoming, the number of houses grew less and less, until they were flying over green fields which rolled out before them like a magical patchwork quilt, sloping gently down towards the sea.

And, finally, they saw Glitter Beach.

The beach looked just as they remembered it from last summer.

Golden
sands carpeted
the bay and swept round
in a huge semi-circle as if hugging
the shimmering sea. Where the sun
touched the sea it seemed as if tiny
silver stars were dancing on the water.
It really was beautiful.

* * *

Glitter Beach was already beginning
to get busy. Fairies were changing
behind towels, skipping back from
the shops with buckets and
spades, setting up stripy
deckchairs and throwing
open the shutters of

ice-cream-coloured beach huts.

The Water Fairies were walking
up and down the beach looking very
glamorous in their bright red costumes
and carrying their inflatable wings.

At the first sign of a fairy in trouble in the water, they could blow up their wings and head out into the sea.

Felicity had never actually seen any of them do this. Every time she had been to the beach they seemed to spend more time sitting on deckchairs by the 'Lost Fairy' sign drinking lemonade and eating ice-cream than rescuing fairies. Still, she was glad they were there.

Daisy and Felicity put up the sun umbrella and they all hung their wings from it. They wriggled into their swimming costumes, then laid their towels out on the sand.

"Last one in the water eats a sandy sandwich!" yelled Felicity, as she raced towards the sea, hotly pursued by Holly and Daisy.

Only Polly remained standing forlornly under the sun umbrella, her legs as wobbly as a jellyfish.

Any moment now, her friends would turn and see her on the beach and come running back to get her.

Carefully, Polly undid her wings, hung them up with the others and, taking a sandwich from the picnic basket, crept away and hid behind one of the beach huts.

"They'll probably think I've gone to buy an ice-cream," she thought.

Felicity made huge splashes when she swam, so her friends tried to keep away from her. Holly swam with her head above the water, for fear of messing up her hair, while Daisy floated on her back, staring at the sky, and was carried along by the waves. After a few moments they realised that Polly was missing.

Daisy was sure that Polly had run into the sea with them.

"At least I *think* I'm sure," she said.

Felicity couldn't remember seeing Polly running down the beach, but thought she had been in the sea with them.

Holly pointed out that none of them would have been able to see whether she was there or not, with the amount of splashing Felicity had been doing!

The fairies' toes still touched the sand on the bottom, even though it felt like they'd been swimming out to sea for ages, so they waded back towards the beach.

"POLLY!" they all shouted. "POLLY, WHERE ARE YOU?"

One of the Water Fairies approached them.

"Is there a problem?" she asked.

"We've lost our friend!" said Felicity. "We thought she might have been back on the beach, but we can't see her."

"Look!" squealed Daisy. "Her wings! Polly's wings are under the umbrella! She'd never go anywhere other than the sea without her wings. She *must* have followed us into the water!"

Holly, who was worried about Polly but was also enjoying the drama, added, "But we don't think she followed us out!"

There was no time to lose. The Water Fairy leapt into action. In an instant, her wings inflated and she

ran towards the sea blowing a small
silver whistle. The other Water
Fairies began to scramble off their
deckchairs and run down the beach
and into the water.

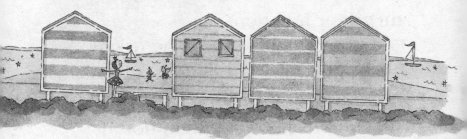

From behind the beach huts, Polly
heard the whistle and popped her
head around the corner. She could
see Holly, Daisy and Felicity huddled
together by the water's edge, and
three Water Fairies flying rapidly
across the beach, their wings
inflating as they flew.

Suddenly she realised what was
happening.

"They think I'm lost at sea and
they're trying to rescue me!"

Polly darted out from behind the

hut and rushed towards her friends.

"I don't need saving!" she cried, running towards them.

The fairies turned towards her. Daisy's curly hair had gone flat, all the colour had gone from Holly's face and 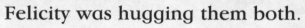 Felicity was hugging them both.

When she saw them, Polly burst into tears.

Felicity could barely get the words out for sobbing. "We thought... we thought you had *drowned*!"

The Water Fairies had noticed Polly return and one of them came up to the huddle of friends.

"Are you alright?" she asked Polly. "Where were you?"

"Hiding behind the beach huts," sobbed Polly, huge tears plopping into the sand.

"Why?" asked Felicity.

It was time to come clean. To own up to her secret. The thing that she had been keeping from her friends for years.

She, Polly, who was good at everything and never failed at anything, had never learnt to swim.

"You can't swim?" said Holly. "I wouldn't worry, lots of fairies are scared of water."

"I'm not scared of *water*," sniffed Polly. "I'm scared of *sinking*!"

Felicity hugged Polly. "Why didn't you *tell us*?"

"Everyone thinks I'm so good at everything, I was scared to admit there was something I couldn't do." Polly was still sobbing.

The Water Fairy put her arm around Polly.

"It's really important to learn how to swim. Even if *you* don't need rescuing, perhaps someone else will!"

"I know," sniffed Polly. "I just don't know where to start!"

"How about a lesson now, here with me on the beach?" said the Water Fairy. "We'll make you a Water Fairy for the day!"

Polly nodded enthusiastically.

And, with that, the Water Fairy handed Polly a pair of inflatable wings and led her into the water.

"Bet you an ice-cream Polly will end up being brilliant at swimming too!" said Felicity, before racing her fairy friends back to their towels.

And, as the three friends stretched out on the sand, under the shimmering sun, they could hear Polly giggling and splashing – happy in the water at last.

good friends won't mind
what you can
and can't do
as long as you're you!

Spooky Sleepover

During the lesson about 'Great Fairies in History', Felicity Wishes began to think about what she was going to do after school.

Tearing a tiny scrap of paper from her exercise book, she scribbled a note and passed it under the desk to Holly, who opened it, nodded, and passed it on to Daisy.

Daisy gave a little thumbs up sign and tried to pass it to Polly, but Polly was enjoying the lesson so much, she didn't

My house, after school for Chocolate cake?

F xxx

notice Daisy pushing the note towards her across the desk.

Miss Fossil, the history teacher, did.

"Daisy, I do hope that note is extra information on the fairies we are studying," she said, picking up the folded piece of paper.

"If only I could grant wishes for myself," thought Daisy. "I could make myself disappear!"

Miss Fossil read the note, raised her eyebrows and, scrunching it into a ball, threw it into the wastepaper basket.

"I take it that you have all finished last week's history homework?" she asked, in a voice which meant she knew they hadn't even started.

"Nine o'clock tomorrow morning I expect to see a large pile of books on my desk!"

History homework! They'd forgotten all about it.

✳ ✳ ✳

Felicity, Holly, Daisy and Polly
huddled together under the large
oak tree in the playing field during
break.

"That was *sooo* embarrassing,"
said Daisy.

"I was looking forward to you all
coming round and eating chocolate
cake," said Felicity. She'd baked the
cake yesterday and, by the time she'd
covered it in thick, dark, gooey icing,
the burnt bits hardly showed at all.

Holly was beginning to panic.

"What about this homework?

I haven't even started it and it's due in tomorrow!"

"Don't get your wings in a twist, Hol," said Felicity, as she reached into her bag and pulled out her exercise book. "All we have to do is write about a famous fairy. It can't be *that* difficult."

After she had removed a piece of bubble gum which was stuck to the cover, shaken out the crumbs from a half-eaten biscuit, and leafed through a dozen doodle-filled pages, Felicity finally found the instructions for their homework.

"Choose one important fairy in history. In your own words, describe why this fairy has made a difference to the lives of modern fairies," read Felicity.

"What are we going to *do*?" shrieked Holly.

Polly, who had been busy reading a book and munching an apple, looked up calmly.

"Go to the school library, find books on fairy history, read them, choose a fairy, then write about her. That's what I did."

Holly, Daisy and Felicity looked at Polly in astonishment.

"You mean," said Felicity, "you've already *done* the homework?"

"Mmmm," mumbled Polly, her mouth full of apple.

"Goody – we can copy it!" said Holly, flinging her arms in the air in relief.

"I've handed it in," said Polly, still munching.

"And you didn't *tell* us?" asked Daisy.

"I knew I couldn't leave it until the

last minute,"
replied Polly.
"I'm out
tonight."
"What!
Where?
Who with?"
chorused
her friends.

"I asked Pearl, one of the Tooth
Fairies, whether I could come out
with her tonight and see a proper
Tooth Fairy in action. I won't be
home until very late."

The other fairies were impressed.
Polly was taking her decision to
become a Tooth Fairy *very* seriously.

Felicity had an idea.

"Why don't we all go the library,
then go back to my house and do
our homework together!"

Daisy wasn't sure.

"If we spend the evening chatting

and eating cake, I don't think we'll have time to finish it. We'll be up all night!"

"Perfect!" cried Felicity. "We can have a sleepover! It won't matter *what* time we finish if you stay at my house."

"Are you *sure* you can't come?" Holly asked Polly, secretly hoping that even though Polly had done her homework, she might be persuaded to stay at Felicity's as well. That way, if they got stuck, Polly could help them.

Polly shook her head. "Count me out. I'll definitely either be too late or too tired to join you."

✳ ✳ ✳

It was so long since any of them had been to the School Library, that Felicity, Holly and Daisy managed to get lost in the corridors and found themselves flying in totally the wrong direction towards Fairy Godmother's office, just as she was flying out.

"What are you young fairies up to?" she asked.

"We're off to the library, Fairy Godmother," said Felicity.

"We want to get on with our history project," added Daisy.

"How lovely," thought Fairy Godmother to herself as she flew off to yet another staff meeting. "What a change to find fairies who are eager to do their homework instead of leaving it until the last minute!"

✳ ✳ ✳

The library shelves were bursting with books on every subject. The fairies stood in a group, looking bewildered.

A crown appeared over the top of a pile of books, followed by a huge pair of glasses. They belonged to Miss Page, the school librarian. Although Miss Page liked the young fairies to enjoy reading, she *didn't* like them messing up her neat shelves by not putting the books they had borrowed back in the right place.

"Could you help us find information on famous fairies?" Felicity asked Miss Page, showing her the homework question.

Miss Page shuddered at the sight of Felicity's crumpled exercise book. She pointed them towards the history shelves.

"*Please* be careful," she pleaded. "Some of those books are *very* old!"

✳ ✳ ✳

Looking through the books, Felicity and her friends found reading about famous fairies much more fun than they had imagined. There were tales of fairies who had made solo flights across the desert or flown to the brightest stars in the sky. They read about a fairy who invented wings which could be powered by sunshine, and a famous fairy poet who always spoke in rhyme, even when she wasn't writing poems!

Felicity decided to write about a fairy called Lucy Sunshine, who had been at the School of Nine Wishes many years ago. Lucy was the first fairy to make powdered summer sun, a vital ingredient in modern sparkle dust. Without Lucy's work, sparkle dust could only be produced in very small quantities.

Daisy was getting very excited reading about famous Blossom Fairies and was scribbling excitedly in her notebook.

"Did you know that the first known Blossom Fairy was called Rose Petal?"

she asked Holly and Felicity. "She was the fairy who discovered the everlasting lily."

Holly was finding it difficult to choose a famous fairy to write about. They were all interesting, but which one had made the most difference to the life of a modern fairy like Holly?

Just then, Holly's mobile phone rang.

Felicity and Daisy gasped and ducked behind the shelves. They were not supposed to use their phones in school and *never* in the library.

Holly tried to turn it off, but it was too late. Miss Page had seen her and, from the way she was flying, Holly knew she was in BIG trouble.

"Please give me that phone," she whispered sharply to Holly. "You can collect it from me this time tomorrow."

"Twenty-four hours without my phone!" whispered Holly. "What *am* I going to do?"

"What did people do before phones?" said Felicity. "Whoever invented them really made a difference to our lives!"

"That's it!" exclaimed Holly. *"That's* who I will write about. The fairy who invented the telephone!"

In the middle of *The History of the Fairy World, Part 3*, they found the inventor of the fairy phone, Scarlet Belle.

"Thank goodness for Scarlet!" they whispered to each other as they pushed the books back on the shelves, gathered up their notes, pens and pencils, and, to the relief of Miss Page, left the library.

✱ ✱ ✱

At Felicity's house, surrounded by chocolate cake and fizzy lemonade, the fairy friends settled down to finish their homework.

Felicity had trouble starting hers. She looked at the question on the

paper and the notes she had made in
the library.

She copied the question neatly into
her exercise book, drew a line under it
and made a smiley face for a full stop.

She chewed on the end of her pen,
rearranged the coloured pencils in
the order of the colours of the
rainbow and watched her friends
scribbling away.

"If Lucy Sunshine can make
powdered summer sun, then surely
I can manage to do my homework!"
thought Felicity, as she began to
write.

By the time they had all finished their homework, it was dark and windy outside and pouring with rain.

"I'm feeling really sleepy," yawned Daisy, who was already in her nightie and was sitting on Felicity's bed, her toes tucked under the pink covers.

"I feel tired too," said Felicity. Her eyelids felt so heavy they needed matchsticks to prop them up.

Felicity and Daisy snuggled down at one end of the bed and Holly tucked herself in at the other. They were too tired to even tickle each other's toes. But the moment Felicity turned out the light, she felt wide-awake.

While the other two slept, Felicity listened to the roar of the wind and the lashing of the rain against the window.

Lying very still, so as not to wake Daisy and Holly, Felicity's gaze rested

on the gap below the blind, where she
could see the moon shining, filling the
room with a misty white light.

Suddenly the moon disappeared,
and the room became pitch black.

Felicity's heart began to beat faster
and faster. Then, from outside, came
a long, low, moaning noise.

"Are you awake?" Felicity whispered
to Daisy, who continued to snore
gently beside her.

Felicity wriggled her toes at the
bottom of the bed and tickled Holly.
"Are you awake, Holly?"

"Mmm…" replied Holly sleepily.

"Can you hear that noise…that
moaning noise?"

"It's just the wind," muttered
Holly, rolling over.

"Holly, listen!" whispered Felicity.
"There's something out there!"

"It's just the wind, Felicity," Holly
said. "Unless… it's The Thing!"

Felicity sat bolt upright in bed.
"What thing?"

By this time Daisy was awake too,
so Felicity switched on the light.

"What's going on?" asked Daisy,
rubbing her eyes.

"Holly said that moaning noise is
a thing," squeaked Felicity.

Holly sat up in bed and pulled the
covers about her.

"Not *a* thing," she said in a low
menacing whisper. "*The* Thing! No
one has ever seen The Thing. But
they know when it's there."

"H-h-h-ow?" gasped Felicity, who
had pulled the covers right up over
her nose so only her scared, wide

eyes were peeping over the top.

"Because it moans and it wails and even the moon hides when it's near!"

Felicity remembered the moon disappearing, and pulled the covers right over her head.

At that moment there was another groaning and creaking sound, like a rusty, old pair of wings.

"Has it gone?" Daisy whispered. "Has The Thing gone?"

Holly was enjoying herself.

"The Thing never leaves. Wherever you hide, The Thing will get you!"

Felicity and Daisy were now really frightened and, even though she had started the story as a bit of fun, Holly also began to feel scared.

"Where does it stay when it's here?" asked Felicity, her voice trembling.

"It's downstairs," squeaked Daisy in a high-pitched whisper. "Listen!"

"It's just a joke," said Holly, her

tummy doing somersaults as she
clutched the bedding around her. "I
mean, I was just pretending. There's
no such thing as The Thing."

But even Holly couldn't fail to miss
the sound coming from downstairs.

Tap. Tap. Tap.

"It's the wind," she said, trying to
convince herself.

"The wind doesn't make that sort
of noise!" said Felicity under her
breath. "It's The Thing!"

The tapping stopped.

Holly sank back on to the bed. The moon seemed to be laughing at her from behind the blind.

"I'm going to pull the blind down tightly and then let's get to sleep," she said, as she tiptoed her way to the window.

Just as she touched the blind – "ARRGHH!" – she leapt back from the window, white as a snowdrop and shaking like a jelly.

"What is it?" cried Felicity.

"Is it The Thing?" screamed Daisy, as Holly dived back under the bedclothes.

"A face... I saw a face..." Holly gasped.

All three friends hid under the covers and hugged each other tightly.

The tapping noise started again, followed by an eerie howl. It seemed to be closer than ever.

Eeeeekk!

Felicity was more frightened than she had ever been in her life, but feeling her friends shaking with fear beside her suddenly made her feel much braver. They needed her to be strong.

"Are you *sure* that you made up the story about The Thing?" she asked Holly in the dark of the bedclothes.

"Y-y-ess," said Holly, her teeth chattering with fright.

Tap Tap Tap went the noise.

It was getter faster and faster.

Felicity slowly poked her head out from under the bedclothes, but kept her eyes tightly shut.

The tapping had suddenly become much louder.

BANG BANG BANG it went.

Finding courage she didn't know she had, Felicity opened her eyes and went over to the window with wobbly legs. Taking a deep breath she flung up the blind. And what she saw there gave her a tremendous shock!

Banging on the window and shouting "Let me in!" was Polly!

✳ ✳ ✳

"There weren't many teeth to collect this evening, so I decided to pop by and join the sleepover!" said Polly, climbing through the window and shaking the rain from her wings.

"I tried to knock on the door downstairs but no-one heard me, so I flew up and tried knocking on the window."

"We didn't hear you," said Felicity, handing her a towel. "We had our heads under the covers!"

"But you saw me, Holly," said Polly. "Why didn't you let me in?"

"She thought you were The Thing," said Daisy.

"My turn to make the hot chocolate, I think!" said Holly, heading towards the kitchen, her cheeks bright pink with embarrassment. "And then you can tell us all about your night, Polly!"

the most scary
thing about
being frightened

is what you

imagine

Cooking Crisis

Felicity Wishes and her friends were making their way home from school. They were talking about the lessons they'd had that day.

Suddenly, Felicity remembered something *much* more exciting.

"Polly! There's only a couple of days left until your birthday and you *still* haven't decided whether or not to have a party!"

Holly, who had been flying along while trying to read a magazine at the same time, crashed into

Daisy, who had stopped to smell some pink roses.

"I've been too busy to even think about my birthday," Polly told Felicity, as she helped untangle Holly and Daisy. "I suppose I should do *something*."

"Leave it to me!" said Felicity brightly. "I'll make you a yummy birthday cake. In fact, *lots* of scrummy birthday cakes!"

The fairies looked at each other with raised eyebrows and wide eyes. It wasn't that Felicity didn't cook. She *loved* to cook. It was just that she never stuck to a recipe! Sometimes she forgot to read the recipe all the way through before starting, or found she didn't have all the ingredients, or forgot to switch the oven on. Something *always* seemed to go wrong.

Felicity saw her friends looking at

her in an 'are you sure this is a good idea?' kind of way.

"Don't worry!" she said. "Come to my house on Saturday at four o'clock for a birthday tea!"

With a hop, skip and a flip of her wings, Felicity flew off to plan Polly's birthday tea.

"I'll pop round early," said Daisy to the others. "*Someone* has got to keep an eye on her!"

* * *

All day on Friday during school, Felicity thought about what she was going to bake.

"Are you *sure* you want to do this, Felicity?" asked Polly, after Felicity had questioned her for the hundredth time about whether she preferred jam or cream, or both, in a sponge cake. "I'm happy to go to Ice-Cream Dreams if it's too much bother."

"It's all under control!" Felicity told Polly, writing down another cake idea on her ever-increasing list.

✳ ✳ ✳

Felicity had taken a big pile of cookery books to bed with her and had marked the recipes with little slips of pink paper. It had taken her ages to fall asleep and, when she finally did, she dreamt she'd fallen into a giant bowl of cake mixture and eaten too much to climb out!

When she woke the next day, not only was it later than she had planned, but all the little pink slips of paper had fallen out of the cookery books, as she'd fallen asleep with them on her bed.

"Never mind," she thought to

herself. "I'm sure I can remember the recipes. I've read them so many times!"

She looked at the list of cakes to bake. She would have to work quickly if she was to get everything finished by four o'clock!

* * *

Felicity switched on the oven.

"I'll leave it to heat up for ten minutes," she thought to herself. "Then I'll start making the chocolate birthday cake."

She wandered out into the garden, just as Holly was flying past. Seeing Felicity, she stopped to chat.

"I'm off to have my hair done,"

said Holly. "I thought I might try Star Treatment for a change."

Holly and Felicity were still chatting about hairstyles when Holly wrinkled her nose.

"Can you smell burning?" she asked Felicity. "Have you got anything in the oven?"

"Not yet," replied Felicity. "I wonder if someone is having a bonfire?"

The burning smell became stronger and stronger.

"Are you *sure* it's not something you're cooking?" said Holly, setting off down the path to Felicity's house.

"It's really not me!" laughed Felicity, following her. "I've nothing in the oven to burn!"

They trooped into Felicity's kitchen. Thick black smoke was pouring from behind the oven door.

"Don't open the door!" shouted Holly. "Turn off the oven and open

the windows!"

Holly and Felicity stood staring
at the smouldering oven. When the
smoke had died down, Felicity
carefully opened the door and
peered inside. Wearing
a huge pair of oven
gloves she reached
in and brought out
a small, black object.

"What is it?" asked Holly, poking it with a wooden spoon.

"I think it *was* a gingerbread fairy. I must have left it in the oven by mistake last time I baked!" said Felicity. "Look, you can just about make out the outline of her crown!"

* * *

Holly left to go to Star Treatment and Felicity began to make the chocolate cake. The oven was still very hot.

"Most people have to wait for the oven to heat up before they start cooking," she thought to herself as she stirred the cake mixture. "Trust me to have to wait for it to cool down!"

The cake mixture was creamy and golden. Time to add the chocolate powder! She looked in the cupboard but couldn't see any.

"I *know* it's in here," she thought as she peered at the tins and packets.

Eventually, at the back, she found
what she was looking for. But, when
she prised open the lid, instead of
seeing a loose mound of chocolate
powder, all she saw was a solid,
brown lump. Felicity looked at the
'Use By' date on the bottom of the
tin. Two years ago!
She tried chipping
away at the lump with
the edge of her
wand, but all she
managed to do was
break a tip off the star.
Hot water didn't even *begin*
to dissolve it, and banging the tin
on the floor to free the chocolate only
dented it.

Felicity glanced at the clock. The
morning was nearly over! There wasn't
time to go to Little Blossoming for
more chocolate powder. She'd have
to turn the mixture into fairy cakes.

She was sure Polly wouldn't mind.

Just as she was about to spoon the mixture into pretty paper cases she decided to add more self-raising flour, just for luck.

* * *

The fairy cake mixture was rising beautifully in the oven, so Felicity began to make the flapjacks.

"Everything is going according to plan!" she thought, as she smoothed the gooey mixture on to two large, silver baking trays.

"This is better," she thought, as she took the golden fairy cakes out of the oven and left them on a rack to cool.

Putting the flapjacks in the oven, she set the timer for fifteen minutes and, as there were no more bowls left to make the cherry cookies, began to do the washing up, her arms elbow deep in frothy bubbles.

Out of the corner of her eye she

noticed something about the rack of
cooling fairy cakes had changed.
Instead of twelve cakes, there were
now only eleven. She was *sure* she had
filled twelve cases, but perhaps she
had been mistaken. A moment later,
she looked again. This time there
were only ten!

Puzzled, Felicity stared at the
cakes. In front of her eyes, one by
one, the cakes rose up and floated
out of the open window and across
the garden.

She had put so much self-raising flour in the mixture they were floating away as they cooled!

Felicity rushed out into the garden and ran down the path, but it was too late. The cakes were heading off over Little Blossoming.

Just when Felicity thought it couldn't get any worse, she remembered the flapjacks. The kitchen timer had gone off, but Felicity had been right at the bottom of the garden, so hadn't heard it!

Dashing back into the house, she opened the oven door and pulled out two trays of solid, burnt flapjacks, stuck firmly to their tins.

Felicity sat at the kitchen table and buried her head in her hands.

"What *am* I going to do?" she wailed.

"Go to the cake shop!" said a voice.

Felicity looked up to see Daisy staring at the chaos that surrounded her distraught fairy friend.

"What are you doing here?" asked
Felicity, drying her eyes on the oven
glove.

"There's a trail of fairy cakes
floating over Little Blossoming," said
Daisy, prodding the burnt flapjacks.
"I guessed they came from your
house."

* * *

Felicity agreed with Daisy that if the
birthday tea was to go ahead, there
was no choice but to go to the cake
shop, but when they arrived at The
Sticky Bun, there wasn't a single cake
to be seen.

"Aren't there *any* cakes left?" Felicity asked the shop assistant desperately.

The assistant shook her head.

"Someone came in and bought every cake, bun and biscuit we had."

* * *

Daisy and Felicity left the shop and sat underneath a huge tree.

Felicity had one last idea.

"Daisy, would you try and wish for some cakes for me?" She hesitated for a moment, remembering her fairy motto. "You would be using your wishes for the good of others."

But Daisy didn't want to try.

"Remember when I tried to magic some scones in cookery class?" she asked Felicity. "They were as heavy and as hard as stones."

Holly claimed her toe still hurt from where a scone had fallen on it.

"Owww!" screeched Felicity.

"Yes, that's what Holly said," remembered Daisy.

"No, I mean, ouch, I've just been hit by a falling apple!"

The fairies looked up and realised they were sitting under an apple tree bursting with apples.

"Toffee apples!" exclaimed Felicity. "We can make Polly toffee apples!"

Daisy flew up into the tree and gently tapped on the branches with her wand, and Felicity stood below, holding out her skirt to catch the falling fruit.

"I don't suppose you've got any lollipop sticks?" asked Daisy.

"Hundreds!" said Felicity, remembering a drawer full of them at home. "I knew they'd come in handy one day!"

* * *

When they got back to Felicity's kitchen they washed the apples, pushed in the lolly sticks and, after checking one of Felicity's recipe books, made a huge pot of sticky toffee mixture into which they dipped the apples.

"Thank goodness *something* has gone right!" said Felicity, admiring the rows of apples dripping with gleaming, glassy toffee.

It was nearly four o'clock! Soon Polly and Holly would be round.

Felicity and Daisy put out Polly's presents and cards on the table and filled jugs with lemonade.

Felicity's tummy began to rumble.

"In all the rush I forgot to have lunch!" she said to Daisy.

"Why not try a toffee apple?" said Daisy. "There are plenty of them!"

Felicity picked up one of the apples and sunk her teeth through the sticky toffee and into the crispy apple. But when she tried to take another bite she found that the toffee was so sticky her teeth had become stuck. The harder she tried to pull the toffee apple from her mouth, the more the toffee set around her teeth.

"Is that nice?" asked Daisy, looking at the apples and not noticing Felicity, wide-eyed and pointing frantically at her mouth.

Felicity let out a muffled noise which sounded like "Mmmmm".

"In that case, I'll try one myself," said Daisy. As she bit into the sticky apple she turned and saw Felicity, her mouth stuck to the toffee apple, trying to tell her not to eat one. Too late!

The fairies tried to pull the apples out but, every time they did, they felt as if their teeth were coming out.

The phone rang. Felicity picked it up.

"Uuh – ho," she said.

"Felicity! It's Polly. I'm going to be a little late. Are you all right?"

Felicity tried to say yes but it came out as "us".

Polly was worried now.

"Is Daisy there? Put me on to Daisy."

Felicity handed the phone to Daisy, who managed to make a series of muffled grunts and snorts before putting the phone down.

* * *

Polly came flying through the door at great speed.

She could not believe her eyes when she saw her two friends sitting at the kitchen table, silent, with two huge toffee apples stuck in their mouths.

As it was Felicity's kitchen and

involved Felicity's cooking, she didn't even ask how it had happened. Very gently, she tugged at the sticky apples in her friends' mouths, ignoring their yelps and carefully chipping away any bits of stuck toffee. Eventually, Daisy and Felicity were freed from their sticky apples.

"You're going to be a brilliant Tooth Fairy!" exclaimed Felicity, gulping down a glass of lemonade. "I thought my teeth were going to be stuck to that toffee apple for ever!"

"Thank goodness I stopped at The Sticky Bun for cakes!" said Holly, coming through the door with a box filled with the most yummy cakes and buns they had ever seen.

TO Polly

"It was *you!*" said Felicity to Holly. "You were the one who bought all the cakes! How did you know that I had had a bad cooking day?"

"I saw the fairy cakes flying across Little Blossoming this morning," said Holly, sticking some candles into one of the cakes. "I thought these might come in useful."

Polly saw Felicity's face crumple a little and put her arms around her.

"Holly buying cakes was a lovely gesture but" – she winked at Holly – "you trying to make them yourself for me is every bit as lovely. It's the thought that counts."

"Don't worry," said Felicity brightly, "I'll have it all under control next year!"

Wand Wishes

The bell for first break rang. Felicity Wishes and her best friends, Polly, Holly and Daisy, flew as fast as they could to get to the sunniest spot on the playing field before anyone else.

They were half-way there, when Felicity remembered she'd left her wand behind.

"You go on without me," she said to her friends. "Save me a spot by the tree – I'll only be a minute."

So the others went on, and Felicity flew back to the Chemistry class where they'd been only minutes before.

The Chemistry teacher, Miss Crystal, was tidying the room, ready for the next lesson. She looked up as Felicity knocked on the door.

"Come in," she said. "What can I do for you, Felicity?"

"Please, Miss Crystal, I think I left my wand here."

"Well," said Miss Crystal thoughtfully. "I haven't *seen* one. Where were you sitting?"

"Just here," said Felicity, walking over to the end of a wooden bench at the front of the room.

"Hmm," said Miss Crystal. "I've already tidied up that area and there was nothing there. Are you sure you left it in here?"

"*Almost* sure," said Felicity, getting down on her hands and knees and looking under the bench. Her tummy was grumbling for her mid-morning Twinkle Bar and she couldn't wait to get out into the sunshine with her friends.

"I suppose I *could* have left it in the hall after assembly," said Felicity, dusting down her stripy tights.

"Well, if it turns up here, I'll let you know. But really, Felicity, you ought to know where your wand is at all times. It might not seem so important now, but when you leave the School of Nine Wishes to become a proper fairy, you'll see how necessary it is to have your wand with you always. It's far better that you get into the habit early on. Now, run along."

Felicity sighed, and looked up at the clock. By the time she'd gone to the school hall to look for her wand,

break would be
nearly over.

"Hmm. Twinkle Bar
or wand-searching?"
she asked herself. It was
a tough decision.

Her tummy grumbled.

"Twinkle Bar it is, then!" she said,
and flew off to join her friends.

"Any luck?" said Polly.

"No, I must have left it in the hall,"
replied Felicity, happily munching
away on her chocolate bar. "I'll go to
lost property after school and see if
anyone's handed it in."

"You can't go a whole day without
your wand!" cried Holly in disbelief.
"You're a fairy!"

"It'll be all right," she said. "I'm
sure we won't have to practise
granting wishes today."

* * *

But it *wasn't* all right. In geography,

when Felicity was asked to stand at
the front of the class and point out
all the countries on the globe
that began with the letter
A, she had nothing
to point with. In
music class, when
it was her turn
to conduct the
recorders, she had
to do it with her finger, and everyone
ended up playing at different times –
and in art class she couldn't believe
it when they were asked to trace
round their wands to make a
picture. Polly lent her hers.

By the time the last lesson was over,
Felicity was desperate for her wand.
She'd never realised how much she
needed it. Wands weren't
just for making wishes,
they were handy for all
sorts of other things.

* * *

"Have you had any wands handed in?" Felicity asked the Lost Property Fairy, Miss Sing.

"Sorry, dear, no. In fact, in all my years as a Lost Property Fairy, I've *never* had a wand handed in!"

"Oh," said Felicity quietly, looking down at her toes.

"It's not the sort of thing a fairy normally loses," explained Miss Sing.

"I know," said Felicity, beginning to feel rather sad. "I don't think I'll *ever* make a proper fairy."

Miss Sing tutted. "We'll have no talk like that, Felicity! One day you'll make a *wonderful* fairy. But not without a wand. Why don't you go

to the new wand shop, Wand Magic?
If you have a really special wand,
you'll *always* want to know where
it is."

Feeling instantly perkier, Felicity
flew off in the direction of the shops.
Shopping, it has to be said, was one
of Felicity's favourite things.

Wand Magic in Little Blossoming had
only been open for a few days, but
already it was said to be the best
fairy wand shop for miles. Even
before you reached it, you could see
the pavement outside glittering. Each
hand-made wand was displayed in a
glass case, on a deep pink, velvet
cushion with gold trimming.

Felicity stood in the doorway, her
mouth wide open in wonder.

"Can I help?" asked the friendly
assistant.

"I'd like a new wand, please," said

Felicity. Then she noticed something. "You've got glitter on your nose!"

"I know, it's working with wands. It gets everywhere! Now, what sort of wand would you like? You look to me like a novice fairy, so I imagine you'll need a Standard Swing. Do you have a handle colour you'd especially like?"

"I was rather hoping for a more special sort of wand – something that I would want to look after properly," said Felicity, who had just spotted some more glitter on the assistant's ear.

"Well," said the assistant, smiling broadly and clapping her hands, "today is your lucky day! Let me just show you this…" and she reached under the counter and took out a small golden key. "Come with me."

Felicity and the assistant left the main shop.

"I wouldn't normally take customers into the stock room, you understand," the assistant said, putting the key into the lock, "but we've just had a delivery of... THESE!"

She threw open the door to reveal a room bathed in the most twinkly silver light Felicity had ever seen. Dozens of beautiful silver starred wands lined the shelves.

Felicity gasped. "They're beautiful!"

"Breathtaking, aren't they? And silver stars – who'd have thought! Gold is such a classic, but these really *are* what you'd call 'more special', I think. And I guarantee you'll be the only fairy in Little Blossoming with a silver starred wand, which really *is* special!"

✳ ✳ ✳

Felicity literally danced out of the wand shop – and she danced all the way home too, waving her silver starred wand as she went. Fairies she passed stopped and stared, some even smiling and waving when they saw her unusual wand.

"This is what it must feel like to be famous," she thought. "I can't wait to show everyone at school tomorrow!"

That night Felicity slept with her
wand under her pillow. In
the morning she carefully
made a little tag for it.

There wasn't a fairy at the School
of Nine Wishes who hadn't heard
about Felicity's wand by the time she
arrived. Excited groups of giggling
fairies kept anxiously turning around
in assembly trying to catch a glimpse
of her spectacular silver wand.

"It's beautiful," sighed Polly. "My
gold wand looks so dowdy in
comparison."

"It's just too sparkly for words,"
said Daisy, putting a hand over
her eyes.

"It's stunning," said Holly reluctantly. Holly always prided herself on being, if not the trendiest fairy, then certainly the one who always got noticed out of the four friends. Felicity had beaten her to it this time.

"Well, you can all have one too," said Felicity. "They had lots in the shop – the delivery had only just arrived. Go on, why don't we *all* get them, then we can match!"

"Yes!" said Polly, excitedly.

"Let's!!" agreed Daisy.

"We can put our old wands away for a rainy day!" said Holly, suddenly cheering up.

* * *

All day Felicity was bombarded with questions by fairies wanting to know about her new silver starred wand.

"How heavy is it?" "Is it easy to wave?" "How did you find it?" "Does its sparkliness get in the way of you seeing things properly?" "Do you know that you've got glitter on your nose?"

Finally the bell sounded for the end of the last lesson, and Polly, Holly, Felicity and Daisy flew straight to Wand Magic. Only, when they turned the corner on to Star Street, they couldn't believe what they saw.

A queue of fairies stretched from the wand shop, past Sugar Twist, the newsagents, past Fresh and Bright, the dry cleaners, past the Post Office, past Ice-Cream Dreams, and finally ended at Sparkles, the café on the corner.

"Goodness," said Polly. "It looks like we're not the only ones who thought about getting a new wand!"

"I don't know if I can queue for all this time, even for something as beautiful as a silver wand like Felicity's," said Daisy, anxiously.

"But I really want one," pleaded Polly.

"And if we *don't* get one, we'll be the only fairies in school without one!" said Holly.

"Well, I don't need to queue," said Felicity, wiggling her wand casually and making them all shield their eyes for a moment. "So I can keep

you supplied with take-away hot chocolates to keep your strength up while you wait!"

When they finally reached the front of the queue for *Wand Magic*, all three fairies had drunk enough hot chocolate to last them for ever.

It was worth it, though, when they found out that they had got the last three sparkly silver starred wands in the shop.

* * *

The next day, the School of Nine Wishes was surrounded by a glittery silver glow that shone for miles. There wasn't a fairy in the school without glitter on her nose. Even Fairy Godmother had a wand that boasted one of the new sparkly silver stars.

"Good morning, fairies," welcomed Fairy Godmother. "Before we begin assembly today, I'd like to introduce you all to a new pupil."

A timid-looking fairy shuffled on to the stage. "This is Tilly, who has just moved to Little Blossoming. I hope you will all do your best to make her feel one of the family at the School of Nine Wishes."

Tilly wasn't in any of Felicity's classes, which Felicity found a little disappointing. She liked to be as friendly as she could, even to people she didn't know, and she had been secretly looking forward to taking the new fairy under her wing.

* * *

It wasn't until lunch-time that Felicity saw Tilly again, quietly sitting alone in the dining hall with her packed lunch.

"Hello there," said Felicity, sitting

down next to her. "I'm Felicity – Felicity Wishes. I saw you in assembly this morning, you're Tilly, aren't you?"

"Yes," said Tilly timidly.

"Would you like to come and eat your lunch with me and my friends? They're ever so nice, I'm sure you'll like them."

Tilly looked up at Felicity, then down at her lunch. She shook her head.

"No… no… no, it's ok," she said, looking awkward.

"Oh, please do! I love making new friends," said Felicity.

"Really, no, I'm afraid I…" and Tilly's eyes welled up with tears. "I'm afraid I'd only embarrass you."

"Tilly!" said Felicity. "What *do* you mean?" and she put her arm round the new fairy's shoulder.

"I- I- I just don't fit in," said Tilly, her voice wobbling with emotion.

"Of course you do," said Felicity comfortingly. "You're a fairy, and that's all you need to be to fit in here."

A large tear rolled down Tilly's face and plopped on to the table.

"No," said Tilly, taking a deep breath. "You don't understand. I really *don't* fit in…"

Tilly rummaged around in her school bag, finally pulling out a

wand with a big golden star on the
end of it. "Look! It's not silver!" she
said, wiping the tear from the table.
"Everyone else has silver stars. I'm the
only one with a gold one. I'll *never*
fit in!" and she buried her head in
her hands and sobbed.

Felicity looked down at Tilly's gold
starred wand, then at her own
beautiful silver starred wand. She
put on her thoughtful look. It was
true, everyone else *did* have silver
stars. She couldn't get another one
from the shop for Tilly because Holly,

Polly and Daisy had taken the last three. There was only one thing to do.

"The only reason I have a silver starred wand is because I lost my gold one," said Felicity. "I was ever so upset when I lost it. Why don't we swap? Gold is more my sort of colour any way – it goes with my hair. Really," she continued, "you'd be doing me a favour. These silver stars have a habit of spreading their glitter everywhere and I'm fed up of brushing it off my nose all the time!"

Tilly took her hands away from her face and looked up. "Really?" she said quietly.

"Really," said Felicity, carefully peeling off her name tag and handing over her wand. "Now, why don't we go and find Holly, Polly and Daisy to have some lunch – I'm starving!"

And, waving their new wands, they flew off to join the others.

it takes a very
special sort of friend

to give away something
they truly treasure

Brilliant Blossoms

It was a beautiful spring day in Little Blossoming. As Felicity Wishes flew through the sparkling golden gates of the School of Nine Wishes, birds were singing, flowers were bursting into bloom and the blue sky was dotted with little clouds so perfect they could have been made out of cotton-wool.

"What a shame to have to go to school on a day like this!" she thought.

Fairy Godmother obviously had the same idea, as she announced

179

that they would all go on a nature flight through Nine Wish Wood when assembly was over.

All the fairies were given a list of plants and flowers to look for on the flight and, excitedly, they set of in groups of four, flying through the wood, weaving in and out of the trees. Daisy flew ahead looking eagerly for the plants on the list: Snowdrop, Crocus, Primrose, Bluebell, Daffodil. Polly, Felicity and Holly followed her, nattering away. Suddenly there was a shout.

"Ow!"

"What's the matter?" asked Daisy, turning to see all three of her friends sitting on the woodland floor rubbing their heads.

"We were too busy chatting and not looking where we were flying," said Felicity, picking leaves out of her crown. "We flew into a tree!"

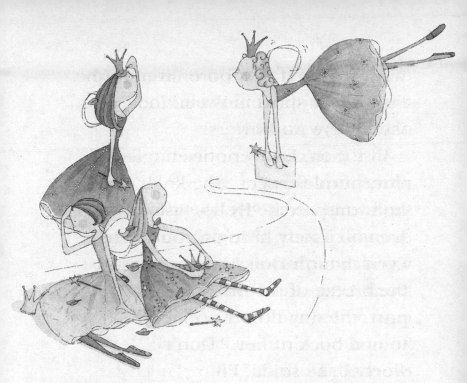

"We've been flying for hours!"
moaned Holly, exaggerating as
usual. "My wings are aching. How
many flowers have you seen, Daisy?"

"None," said Daisy, looking down
at the list.

"Not one?" asked Polly, raising her
eyebrows.

"Not even a single petal," sighed
Daisy, checking her list again.

The fairies looked around Nine

Wish Wood. It was bare. Even in the little sunlit spots between the trees, there were no flowers.

Just then, Daisy noticed a single, tiny, purple crocus. She knelt down and whispered, "Hello, little crocus. Are you lonely here on your own?" Even though Daisy knew it was just the breeze of the other fairies flying past, the tiny flower seemed to nod back at her. "Don't worry," she said. "I'll think of something!"

✳ ✳ ✳

None of the fairies had managed to find any of the things on the list, though plenty of them now had dirty shoes, muddy hands and holes in their tights. Still, it was much more fun than sitting in a classroom all morning.

Daisy had spent the whole day since they got back to school thinking

about the lonely crocus in the wood –
and now she had a plan.

At the last bell of the school day,
as all the fairies streamed out of the
school gates giggling and laughing,
Daisy stayed behind.

With quivering wings she made
her way to Fairy Godmother's office.
The door was slightly open and Daisy
peeped round the corner. The room
was very large and the walls were
lined with antique wands and shelves
bursting with huge books, with titles
such as *The Story of the Modern Wish*
and *The Art of Caring for Your Wings*.

Fairy Godmother was resting in a
large golden chair with her feet on
the desk, flicking through a pile of
holiday brochures. She was planning
a visit to Fairy World. 'A Week of
Carefree Magic' boasted the front of
the brochure.

When Fairy Godmother still didn't

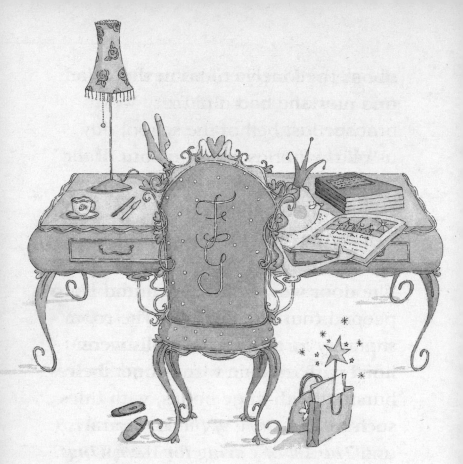

notice her, Daisy gave a little cough.
Fairy Godmother looked up so
sharply and tried to take her legs off
the desk so quickly, her chair tipped
backwards and her crown fell off her
head. Straightening her crown and
reaching for her shoes, she asked
Daisy to come in. Daisy noticed that

she slipped a pile of homework she was marking over the Fairy World brochure.

With a face as red as a rose, Daisy told Fairy Godmother about the lonely, purple crocus.

"I have to admit, I hadn't realised just what a poor state Nine Wish Wood was in," said Fairy Godmother. "None of last year's fairies were the slightest bit interested in plants and flowers. They didn't like to get their hands dirty."

"I LOVE getting my hands in the soil," said Daisy excitedly. "Blossom Fairies don't worry about clean hands!"

"So you'd like to be a Blossom Fairy when you leave school?" Fairy Godmother said, smiling kindly at the embarrassed young fairy in front of her.

"More than *anything*," said Daisy.

"Could I plant some flowers in the wood? I'd make sure they were the sort of flowers which should grow in a Fairy Wood."

Fairy Godmother was very tired. It had been a long day and she just wanted to go home, have a long, hot bubble bath and plan her holiday.

"As long as you promise to tell someone when you are going into the wood and don't disturb the soil too much," she told a delighted Daisy.

* * *

When Daisy got home, she reached under her bed and pulled out a pile of *Glorious Fairy Gardens* and *Magical Garden Makeovers* magazines. These were her favourite types of magazine and she spent hours reading them. When the other fairies had started to tease her gently about "starting to look like a flower" if she read them any more, she began tucking them inside copies of *Fairy Girl*.

In the back of one of the copies of *Magical Garden Makeovers*, in amongst the advertisements for magic beans, green finger hand cream and gardening wands with rosewood stems, she found the advertisement she had been looking for.

Woodland Wonders
Create the perfect display of wonderful
Woodland Wonders flowers in no time at all.
Suppliers of Magical Bulbs
and Seeds to fairies worldwide.
Just sprinkle with morning dew and
success is GUARANTEED!

It was perfect!

＊ ＊ ＊

The wooden box filled with magical bulbs and seeds arrived a few days
later. There were golden seeds so tiny you could mistake them for sparkle dust; larger oval-shaped seeds that seemed to change colour the longer you held them in your hand; bulbs which looked like fat paper pebbles, and one that looked like one of the fairy cakes that Felicity had burnt in cookery class last term.

Taking the seeds to her greenhouse, Daisy carefully filled some seed trays with earth, made tiny holes with the end of her wand and, in each hole, planted a different seed. She gently brushed the earth over the top, before patting it down with the star on the end of her wand. Almost as soon as she began to water the trays with

189

distilled morning dew, tiny green shoots began to appear, just as the advert had promised.

"Magic!" said Daisy, out loud to herself.

* * *

The moment she woke up the next morning, Daisy rushed out of bed and ran down to the greenhouse to see how her seedlings were getting on. She didn't even get dressed.

"Good morning!" she said to them, as she filled up her watering can.

"How are you today?" she asked, as she inspected their leaves.

* * *

For the next week, Daisy spent every spare moment she had in the greenhouse with her Woodland Wonders, watering, whispering and occasionally singing words of encouragement to the growing green shoots, which were getting

bigger every day. Some
of them had now got
so big that Daisy was
able to plant them
out in proper
pots.

One morning, while Daisy was
deep in conversation with one of the
smallest flowers, Felicity popped her
head round the greenhouse door.

"Hello! We're all off to Polly's for tea
and cake," she said. "We wondered if
you wanted to come – we've hardly
seen you lately – but it sounds as if
you've got someone with you."

Daisy giggled.

"That was me talking to my flowers
to help them grow strong enough for
when I…" Daisy stopped. She had
decided that the magical Woodland

Wonders would be a surprise, not only for the lonely, purple crocus but for her friends as well. "...For when I leave them to come and have a large slice of cake at Polly's!"

As Daisy went into the house to wash her hands, Felicity smiled and raised her eyes to the sky.

"Blossom Fairies," she said, shaking her head. "They're all the same."

* * *

The day had come for Daisy to plant the woodland garden.

She had planned to take the plant pots to the wood, but they were too heavy and she would have to make several trips. So, instead, she carefully dug around the plants with her special silver trowel and, being careful not to disturb the roots, put them into a basket.

As she left the greenhouse she felt a bit sad. It seemed very bare. Just

rows and rows of pots with only their
labels to show there had ever been
anything there. She would miss
looking after them. Still,
the woodland garden
would look
fabulous.

   So she set
off to Nine Wish
Wood to begin a happy afternoon
of planting.

* * *

Having had no success trying the
doorbell, Felicity and Polly looked
round the back of Daisy's house.
Daisy had been so busy in her garden
recently, they had decided to surprise
her and take her to Sparkles for a hot
chocolate.

"The greenhouse door is open," said
Polly. "She's probably in there having
a good natter to her plants."

"That's strange. Daisy usually has
the door closed to keep it warm," said
Felicity, becoming worried.

But when they arrived at the
greenhouse door, all they saw were
empty plant pots and soil covering
the floor.

"Oh no!" shrieked Felicity. "Look at
Daisy's greenhouse. It's ruined!
Someone has taken all Daisy's plants!"

"Who in Little Blossoming would do

a thing like that?" said Polly.

Felicity looked at some of the plant labels. Yellow Sparkle Primrose, Sunshine Daffodil, Musical Bluebells, Spotted Orchid.

"We can't let Daisy see this, she'll be heartbroken," she said. "You know how important Daisy's plants are to her."

"What are we going to do?" Polly asked Felicity.

"Look, these are the plant labels, let's see if we can replace the plants before Daisy notices."

So Polly and Felicity flew quickly to the Roots 'N' Shoots garden centre. After explaining to the assistant why they were in such a rush, the assistant left her half-eaten sandwich and copy of *Fairy Girl* on the counter and went to help them match up plants with the labels Felicity had taken from the pots. In no time at all they had the plants they were looking for.

* * *

It took the fairies three flights between the garden centre and Daisy's house to transfer all the plants. There was no time to waste!

Eventually they finished. The greenhouse was full of plants once more.

Felicity and Polly left Daisy a note to meet them in Sparkles. After all that work, they needed a hot chocolate more than anything!

Just as they were scraping the last little bits of cream from the bottom of their glasses, Daisy flew in with a smile as sparkly as a star.

"Thank goodness you two are still here!" she said, sitting down with a thump. "I need a double creamy chocolate shake right now! I've had such a surprise!"

And Daisy began to tell her fairy friends the whole story: about the conversation with Fairy Godmother, about the advert, the magic seeds and how sad she had been to see them go,

and finally how happy the purple crocus had looked when she had surrounded it with a woodland garden.

"But that's not all!" said Daisy, her eyes as wide as saucers. "I got home just now to find that those magic seeds really *are* magic. All the pots that were empty are now full again! I was telling the flowers on the way to the forest how much I would miss them, and now I can see them every day at home!"

Felicity nudged Polly and Polly winked at Felicity, but Daisy was too excited to notice them, or their unusually dirty hands...

Sporting Stars

Fairy Godmother was beginning
her announcements for the school
week.

"For those of you who have a
musical twinkle in your heart, you
will be pleased to know that Miss
Jingle will be starting a recorder
club on Tuesday," said Fairy
Godmother. "Meet after school
under the large oak tree in the first
playing field."

Felicity Wishes was sitting at the
back of the assembly hall, casually

plaiting Holly's hair until Miss Crystal, the science teacher, gave her a 'you know you shouldn't be doing that' sort of look.

"Flying Club is cancelled on Wednesday lunchtime," continued Fairy Godmother. "As most of you know, Miss Fluttering is still in hospital following her unfortunate accident last week."

The fairies giggled. They had noticed that the flagpole had been mended.

"Finally, young fairies," she announced, "I'm sure you don't need reminding to bring a sports kit with you tomorrow for School Sports Day."

Excited fairy noises rippled around the hall.

Fairy Godmother clapped her hands for silence and the fairies all held their wands in their right hands and recited the Fairy Motto, before flying out of the school hall. They were so excited they could hardly fly straight.

"Sports Day!" said Felicity. "Hearts will win this year. I can feel it in my wings!"

"Nonsense," said Holly, grabbing Polly's hand and raising it triumphantly in the air. "Stars always win!"

There were three houses at the School of Nine Wishes: Hearts, Stars and Flowers. Felicity was in Hearts, Holly and Polly were in Stars and Daisy was in Flowers.

Polly was taking sports day very seriously.

"Stars will definitely win this year," she said. "I've been training with weighted wands. Not only will it come in useful for lifting up those heavy pillows when I become a Tooth Fairy, it means no-one will beat Stars in the tug of war!" Polly pushed up her sleeves and flexed her muscles. The other fairies doubled up in fits of giggles. "I'd hate to think what your muscles looked like *before* your training!" squealed Holly. "Don't be so sure that Stars are going to win, Pol," said Felicity. "Now is the time to tell you that I have been secretly practising my Front Flutter Twist every night before I get into bed. In fact," she continued, "it's *how* I get into bed."

The Front Flutter Twist was one of the most difficult wing strokes a fairy could achieve, and the most exciting event at Sports Day. In flying lessons, Miss Fluttering had made the fairies draw endless diagrams, answer hundreds of questions and take two written tests before they were even allowed to attempt it. If you got it wrong, you could sprain your wing so badly you might never fly straight again.

To the gasps of the class, Felicity was what Miss Fluttering called "a natural". What Felicity had never admitted to anyone was that she hadn't meant to attempt it in the first place. Having spent too long in the changing rooms doing her hair,

she had dashed on to the playing
field late, tripped up into the air,
tried to regain her balance and
landed, amazingly, on her feet.

* * *

The next day the fairies gathered on
the tennis courts, nervously chattering
and giggling and crowding round to

look at the list of names and events pinned to the fence. Fairies who weren't huddled round the lists were warming up with some last minute exercises, or frantically calling out for lost plimsolls or a spare wand for relay practice.

Fairy Godmother sounded a large bell for the start of the games.

As neither Felicity nor her friends were due to compete until later, they decided to watch the Single Circuit Freestyle Dash.

Jostling for a front row position near the finishing line, they waited excitedly for Miss Meandering, the geography teacher, to wave her wand for the start of the race.

Holly nudged Felicity and pointed at the fairy in the Star T-Shirt at the start line. It was Amelia, one of the sportiest fairies at the School of Nine Wishes.

"I told you Stars were going to win," she whispered to Felicity, who had noticed with horror that her Housemate, Tilly, was racing against Amelia.

"With Tilly running for Hearts it will be close," said Felicity, not entirely confidently. She wasn't sure that Tilly, who wanted to be a Dream Fairy, would even make it off the starting line, let alone reach the finishing one.

"Who's flying for Flowers?" asked Daisy, craning her neck to see the flyers lining up.

"No-one who can beat Stars!" said Holly.

All eyes were glued to the three nervous fairies waiting to race. A hush settled on the crowd and, in the bright sunshine, Miss Meandering lifted her wand high above her head and said loudly, "Ready...Steady...FLY!" As she brought her wand down with a swoop, the fairies were off.

To everyone's amazement, Tilly was first off the line with the fastest Forward Flapping the girls had ever seen.

Amelia, with an impressive Back Flutter, quickly caught up with her but coming up on the inside lane was the fairy from the Flower team, gliding along as easily as a boat slipping through water.

"STARS!" yelled Polly at the top of her voice.

"HEARTS!" shouted Felicity as loudly as she could.

"AMELIAAAAAAAAAAAAAA!" cried Holly.

"TILLYYYYYYYY!" screamed Felicity.

It was close. Hearts and Stars were within a wing tip of each other, with one corner to turn before the final fly to the finishing line. The atmosphere was electric. Fairies shouted encouragement as loudly as they could.

Stars were in the lead as Amelia raced towards the finish, but Tilly, who looked as if she was beginning to run out of wing power, suddenly got another burst of energy and, spurred on by the cries from the crowd, increased the speed of her Forward Flap to bring her within a

whisper of Amelia. Just as it seemed
Tilly might take over, the fairy from
the Flower team put all she had into
her quiet glide and crept over the
finishing line.

Flowers had won.

"Yippeee!" squealed Daisy, clapping her hands.

"It's just one race," Holly reminded her.

Polly went off to get changed for the Tug of War and Holly, Daisy and Felicity stood looking up at the results board that Fairy Godmother was filling in.

"Stars have won the Wing Assisted High Jump!" said Daisy.

"Hearts have won the Flying Leap!" cried Felicity.

Holly couldn't believe her eyes. "Flowers are in the lead – look!"

"It's very close – and it's not over yet!" said Felicity. "Let's go and see Polly's pillow-lifting muscles in action!"

✳ ✳ ✳

The fairies lined up eagerly by the side of the spectator section for the Tug of War. Polly spotted her fairy friends in the crowd and waved.

"GO ON, POLLY!" they chorused.

"Oh no!" said Felicity. "Who shall I shout for? Polly is tugging against

Hearts! Do I shout for Polly or do I cheer for Hearts?"

"Call for both!" suggested Daisy. "That way, whoever wins, you can't lose!"

When the wand had been waved and the fairies started to tug, Felicity took it in turns to call for her friend and for her team. "Pollyyy!... Heartssss... Pollyyyyyy... Heartssss!"

Polly certainly *had* been practising with weighted wands, and it wasn't long before the fairies from Hearts were on the floor. Stars had won!

* * *

The day had been exhausting. Most of the events had taken place by now and fairies with croaky voices and uchy legs bounced with the little energy they had left up to the results board. It was even closer than before.

"Hearts are only one point behind Flowers!" shrieked Felicity, as she ran off to get changed.

"Stars are only two points behind!" said Holly.

"Whoever wins the final event will win the whole day for their team!" gasped Polly.

The final event of the day was the Front Flutter Twist. All the fairies from the School of Nine Wishes formed a semi-circle around the soft sand area where the Twist would be performed. Each fairy had only one chance to get it right. The fairy who gained the most height with tight control would win four points. *Everything* rested on this event.

✳ ✳ ✳

Fastening her hair with her lucky slide (the same one she had used on the day she had done the Twist when she tripped in flying class), Felicity took a deep breath. It was her chance to win for her team. She knew she could do it.

She was just about to leave the changing room when she heard a noise. It sounded like sobbing. It was coming from the gym cupboard.

"Hello?" she called out. "Are you alright?"

"Not really," sniffed the little voice.

Felicity peeped round the door, but all she could see were piles of netballs and skipping ropes.

"Why don't you come out and tell me what's the matter?" asked Felicity gently.

But the sniffing fairy refused to come out – or let Felicity come in.

"I'm doing the Front Flutter Twist, y-y-you see."

"Are you nervous?" asked Felicity.

"I'll lose. I *always* lose! Now I'm going to lose it for the entire team!" The sound of sniffing behind the netballs got louder.

"It doesn't matter," said Felicity gently. "Fairy Godmother has always said that it's not about the winning, it's about the taking part and trying your best."

"I know..." said the sobbing voice, "but once, just once, it would be nice not to come last."

"If there is one thing I've learnt at the School of Nine Wishes it's that you have to really believe you can do something," said Felicity encouragingly. "If you believe you can do it, then you will!"

"B-b-b-but I *can't* d-d-do it!" sobbed the fairy.

"Of course you can! Believe you can win. Promise me when you go out there, just before you do your Twist, that you'll close your eyes and say to yourself *I can, I can*, over and over."

"If you really think it will help," said the little voice in the cupboard.

"I'm sure of it. Good luck!" said Felicity, as she turned to leave the changing room.

✳ ✳ ✳

Outside, the sun beat down. The three competing fairies stood in front of Fairy Godmother. Felicity looked sideways at the fairy on the Flower team, who was blowing her nose with a spotted hankie.

Fairy Godmother cleared her throat.

"Fairies. As you know, the scores are *very* close. The result of this Twist will determine which house

will win! First prize is the school cup.
Second prize is the school medal, and
the runners-up will all receive a pink
rosette. Could the fairies from each
team take their place?"

A nervous hush descended on the
school. Fairy Godmother raised her

wand. Felicity glanced at the crowd, at her friends, and at the fairy in the Flowers team, who was talking to herself under her breath.

"Ready...Steady...FLUTTER!" cried Fairy Godmother, swooping her wand.

All three fairies bent their knees, straightened their backs and flung themselves forward, fluttering their wings as they twisted.

The crowd gasped as they saw the fairy from the Flowers team twist high above Felicity and the fairy from Stars, then land with perfect precision.

Felicity managed a perfect Front Flutter Twist but didn't gain as much height as the fairy from Flowers, and the fairy from Stars landed in a crumpled heap in the sand.

It was all over in the fluttering of a wing.

Flowers had won!

Fairies ran from all directions on to the sand to give their team members a hug.

"Flowers won!" said Polly. "I don't believe it! I was so sure that Felicity would win this event!"

"How strange," said Daisy. "I wonder why she didn't get as high as she usually does?"

Holly went over and patted Felicity's back. "I'm sorry you lost," she said.

Just then a crowd of fairies from the Flowers team flew past, carrying the fairy from the gym cupboard high above their heads. She was smiling the biggest smile Felicity had ever seen.

Felicity waved and smiled.

"What do you mean, lost?" said Felicity, linking arms with her friends. "I've won a wonderful pink

rosette that will match my stripy
tights perfectly. Now, how about
an ice-cream to finish the day off
properly?"

Chemistry Catastrophe

The alarm went off at 7am. Felicity Wishes woke up, rolled over, and opened one eye just enough to see the clock to turn it off, before snuggling back under her warm, pink duvet.

Every night she went to bed with the intention of getting up early and getting to school on time and every morning when her alarm went off she changed her mind.

"Why is it," she thought sleepily, "that beds seem so unappealing when it's time to go to bed and so appealing when it's time to get up? Life would be so much easier if it were the other way around!"

Felicity reached out from under the covers to pick up the school timetable from her bedside table. Double Science followed by Practical Wish-Making. She loved going to the School of Nine Wishes and seeing her friends but somehow, despite her best intentions, her lessons never went according to plan. In her last end of term report, Fairy Godmother had written: "Felicity Wishes is a delightful fairy, popular with her classmates, polite and helpful. However, she *must* try to concentrate more in class."

Felicity pulled the covers over her head as she thought back to the start of school. Things had begun well, but had rapidly gone downhill...

On the first day of the first term in the very first lesson it had all looked so promising. Fairy Godmother welcomed them.

"Young fairies," she boomed. "Welcome to the School of Nine Wishes. I hope you will all be very happy here. Now, who can tell me why you are here?"

Felicity instantly put up her hand. She knew the answer. She was quite beside herself, she actually knew the answer!

Fairy Godmother was delighted to see such a keen young fairy.

"What's your name, dear?" she asked.

"Felicity," said Felicity proudly. "Felicity Wishes."

"So, Felicity Wishes, tell the class why you are here at the School of Nine Wishes."

"Because," said Felicity, "we got

a letter telling us to come."

A slight giggle rippled through the classroom. Fairy Godmother struggled to keep a straight face and paused before composing herself. "That's true, Felicity," she said. Felicity was just about to beam with delight that she had got the answer right when Fairy Godmother added, "but it wasn't quite the answer I was looking for. Can anyone else help?"

Felicity's friend Polly put her hand up and said, "We're here to learn all the skills we need to become fully qualified fairies,

so that we can go out into the world and use our magical powers for the good of others."

"Beautifully put!" said Fairy Godmother, clapping her hands. "That, young fairies, in a nutshell, is why you are all here!"

Felicity didn't hear anything else Fairy Godmother said after that. Her cheeks were burning hot with embarrassment and she hung her head so low her crown nearly fell off.

"How awful!" she said to Daisy, after the class. "I must have set some kind of school record for getting the answer wrong to the first question of the first lesson of the first class on the first day of the first term!"

"You didn't get it *wrong*, Felicity," said Daisy.

"I didn't get it *right*," mumbled Felicity, "or why did Fairy Godmother put the question to the class again?"

"It just wasn't the answer she was looking for, that's all," said Daisy. "It's nothing to worry about."

But Felicity *was* worried. How did you know what answer was required if there wasn't always a right one or a wrong one?

After finally managing to drag herself out of bed, Felicity sat down to eat her breakfast. She thought about her school report again.

"Concentrate more, that's the key," she said to herself, wiping the milk moustache from her mouth. The problem was, it was so easy to get distracted!

* * *

After school assembly, where the fairies sang like angels only much better, Felicity, Polly, Holly and Daisy trooped off to the science lab.

Inside, there were row upon row of shimmering glass test tubes in holders, carefully labelled bottles of every colour sparkle you could imagine, shiny silver spatulas, pots of coloured crystals with names such as Frosted Juniper, Preserved Snowflakes and Star Dust. The science teacher, Miss Crystal, moved from desk to desk ticking off the items on her clipboard. This was obviously going to be a special science lesson!

"Fairies!" she announced. "Today, we are going to have our first attempt at making magic sparkle dust." The room buzzed with excitement. This was a taste of what they had come to school for – to learn how to be proper fairies.

"Settle down, settle down!" said Miss Crystal, laughing. "Those of you who manage to get some useable dust can take it into your next class for your practical wish lesson."

Even *more* exciting! Making sparkle dust and then actually being able to use it!

Miss Crystal continued, "Everything you need is on the workbench. We're only going to make quite weak sparkle dust as this is your first attempt. The instructions are clearly written out for you. See how you get on and let me know if there is a part you don't understand."

Felicity looked at the instructions. They made absolutely no sense to her at all.

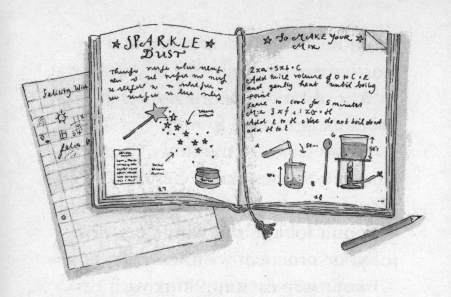

Felicity looked around her.

Everyone else seemed to be counting out spatulas of powder and measuring liquids into test-tubes already. There was much sniffing and stirring and pouring and shaking and watching and waiting. Miss Crystal had told them to ask if they didn't understand something, but how could Felicity confess that she didn't understand ANYTHING?

Polly was waiting for her mixture to boil. Out of the corner of her eye, she noticed Felicity looking like a startled rabbit.

"Are you alright, Felicity?" she asked her puzzled friend.

"I have NO IDEA what to do, Polly," said Felicity, wrinkling her nose. "No idea even where to start!"

"Don't look at the whole equation – it looks really scary at first," said Polly. "Take it step by step. Start with two spatulas of the stuff in bottle A and five spatulas from the jar labelled B. That makes a mixture Miss Crystal is calling C."

Suddenly it all seemed to make sense! It was just like following a recipe.

Felicity had spent so much time worrying, she was now very behind. She'd have to rush to catch up.

First she picked up a bottle of the most beautiful white powder. This was made from pressed and dried frost crystals, and looked good enough to eat. She quickly mixed the powder with some preserved star dust and added a little morning dew. There was no time to measure. She'd just have to guess.

Felicity glanced over her shoulder. Everyone else looked as if they had almost finished.

"Oh goodness," she thought, turning back to her beaker. "Did I add the morning dew already?"

She'd been so busy looking to see what everyone else had been doing, she'd forgotten what she'd done herself.

"Another one for luck," she said hopefully, as she poured some more morning dew into her beaker and gave it another stir. She popped the glass beaker on the pink tripod and began to heat the mixture. Nothing happened.

"A watched beaker never boils," she told herself, as she started to mix up the next set of ingredients. The mixture turned the most beautiful shade of twinkly blue.

She turned back to her glass beaker on the tripod. Still it wouldn't boil. The others had already poured their mixtures on to glass plates and were waiting for them to cool. Miss Crystal was busy talking to the other fairies and didn't seem to notice Felicity scowling at her still lukewarm mixture.

"Is everyone alright?" called Miss Crystal, above the noise of the class.

"Yes, Miss Crystal!" came back the reply.

"No, Miss Crystal!" muttered Felicity, under her breath.

Felicity decided there was nothing for it but to turn up the heat on the Bunsen burner. The flame roared and soon the golden liquid began to bubble furiously. Excellent! If she *really* hurried she would finish by the end of class and still have some sparkle dust to take to the next lesson.

Felicity looked at the notes: Leave to cool for five minutes. She didn't have time to wait for five minutes. She tried blowing on the liquid, but the steam blew back in her face and made her cough. Perhaps if she poured some out into another flask, that would help it cool down.

She carefully poured some of the steaming liquid into a clean flask. It still seemed very hot. Time was running out. The others were scraping up their golden crystals and spooning them into tiny silk bags.

Daisy and Polly came over to see how Felicity was getting on.

"I'm nearly finished," she said brightly. "All I've got to do is add some of these blue crystals to this golden mixture and I'm there!"

"No, Felicity!" said Polly in a slight panic. "You have to add the golden liquid to the blue crystals.

Not the other
way round!"

But Felicity didn't hear her. She had
already begun to add the blue crystals
to the still hot flask of golden liquid.
There was the most tremendous
gurgling sound, like someone
burping over and over again.

"EVERYONE DUCK!"
shrieked Polly, who,
with Daisy, had
crouched under
the bench.

Suddenly the mixture let out the loudest burp of the lot and a cloud of green bubbles emerged like an erupting volcano from the flask. Green bubbles began to fill the classroom. No-one could see anything of Felicity other than the top of her pink crown.

Miss Crystal rushed to open the window and the bubbles floated out of the classroom and up and away across the playing fields.

Felicity stood dripping wet and bright green from the liquid sparkle dust.

After making sure that it was only Felicity's pride that was hurt, Miss Crystal sent everyone to the cloakroom to clean themselves up. She asked Felicity to stay behind. Felicity was now weeping, huge tears plopping gently on to the bench.

"What happened, Felicity?" asked Miss Crystal gently.

Felicity was sobbing and sniffing at the same time. She didn't have a hanky and couldn't even wipe her nose on her dress because it was covered in stuff which had begun to dry to a green powder which made her sneeze. Miss Crystal gave Felicity her white lace hanky. Felicity blew her nose, wiped her eyes and sobbed. "I didn't know what I was doing at

first and I didn't like to ask. Then
I thought I knew what I was doing
and didn't need to ask. Then I did
what I needed to do so quickly that
I didn't know what I was doing. And
now everyone knows what I've done!"

"I see," said Miss Crystal, who
didn't really see at all but guessed
that Felicity had overheated her
mixture, not let it cool and muddled
up the mixtures at the beginning and
the end. The young fairy looked so
sad it was impossible to be cross.

"Perhaps," thought Miss Crystal to
herself, "I should have paid more

attention to everyone in the class.
It's a lesson for me too."

"I don't have any sparkle dust to
take to the next class," said Felicity
sadly. "That's two classes ruined!"

Miss Crystal pulled out a large
silver key which was hanging
on a long silver chain around
her neck. She walked over
to a small plain cupboard
on the wall and unlocked
it. Suddenly the entire room
was filled with a glittery
glow. Inside the cupboard
were rows and rows of glass
bottles. There was a huge bottle
labelled Sparkle Dust Practice Grade
I, a smaller bottle marked Sparkle
Dust Grade II, a very small bottle
labelled Super Sparkle Dust – Double
Strength, and several others that
Felicity couldn't read. There seemed
to be enough sparkle dust to make

wishes for everyone in the world!

Felicity was open-mouthed with wonder.

"This cupboard is our secret," Miss Crystal said, spooning some dust into one of the little silk bags.

"But won't everyone wonder where I got it from, when science class has just ended so badly?" asked Felicity.

"If anyone asks you where you got it, just tell them it came from your science class and leave it at that. Now, off you go."

Felicity had just got to the door when Miss Crystal called out.

"Felicity! Next time, try to concentrate – and if you get in a muddle, don't be afraid to ask."

And, ever since then, Felicity has always asked, even though she sometimes thinks her questions seem silly. After all, she doesn't want to risk ruining another dress!

it's better to feel silly and ask when you're not sure

than look silly when you don't!

Spotlight Solo

It was the most exciting event of the school year at the School of Nine Wishes: the annual School Concert.

Fairy Godmother had announced the date weeks ago during assembly.

"Young fairies," she boomed to the crowd of eager young faces, their wings quivering with anticipation, "the school concert will be held three weeks from today. Organise yourself

into groups. Each group will have
five minutes in which to entertain
the audience."

Holly was beside herself.

"My chance to show what I can
do!" she said to her friends, as they
huddled together at first break to
discuss what they were going to do.
She took a deep breath and
announced, "I can smell stardom
already!"

"That's the school dinners cooking,"
said Felicity, wrinkling her nose.

Polly butted in. "Are we going to do

this together as a group, or not?" she asked her friends.

Holly tossed her hair, put her hands on her hips and said with a flourish, "I have to do a solo. I just have to. It's my big chance to be..." she paused, looked up at the sky and said in a ridiculously husky voice, "noticed."

The other three dissolved into giggles. Holly was so over the top. If she was like this three weeks before the performance, what would she be like on the actual day?

Polly would be quite content painting scenery or helping the others learn their lines, so she was very happy to leave the spotlight to Holly. "Don't worry," she said, "you'll get your solo spot. Now, what else are we going to do with our five minutes of fame?"

Daisy said she'd written a poem

entitled, 'The Magic of Flowers', which, if the others agreed, she'd like to read aloud. The others thought this was a good idea, even Holly, who was still planning her own solo act.

"After all," she thought, "it's down to star quality."

The fairies decided that the best plan was for Daisy to read her poem first, then all four of them would perform a dance routine to a song that they would write together. Holly could sing a solo verse in the middle, then they would all join in for the final verse. Polly didn't like the thought of being on stage on her own, and Felicity didn't seem to mind one way or the other, as long as she was with her friends, so it seemed like the perfect solution.

Writing the song proved rather more
   difficult.

   Dreamy Daisy wanted
something soft and gentle with
a nice tune. Polly thought that
anything that didn't give Daisy a fit
of the giggles would be a start.
Felicity wanted something disco so
she could wear her spangly skirt
and do star jumps, and Holly – well,
Holly thought that if she was going
to sing the solo it was only fair for
her to choose the style she felt most
comfortable with. Which was opera.
The others groaned.
   The four friends sat looking at
the white piece of paper in front of

them. They'd been going round in circles for ages and still couldn't decide.

"Let's be sensible," said Polly. "Do any of us play any musical instruments?" Polly saw Felicity's mouth begin to open and quickly added, "Other than the recorder?"

The fairies agreed that their skills were limited. Neither opera nor disco was exactly suited to the recorder, and dancing with a recorder in your mouth would definitely end in tears.

"So," Polly continued, "we've got limited musical ability and we have to write a song. Can I suggest that we choose a tune we all know and write some words to go with it? How about using the melody to 'Twinkle Twinkle Little Star'?"

Felicity thought this was a lovely idea. Daisy was so tired from giggling she would agree to anything. Holly

was already working out how she
could transform the simple tune into
something fit for a fairy diva.

The three weeks since Fairy
Godmother had announced the date
of the concert had flown by and there

were now only twenty-four hours to go. It was time for the first full dress rehearsal!

All day, fairies had been rushing about with paints and paintbrushes, glitter and sequins, pins and needles, instruments, scripts and sheets of music. From inside classrooms came the sound of fairies singing, performing sketches, squeaky scale practice, nervous laughter and frantic cries for lost scripts. If you listened carefully, you could even hear one brave fairy practising her jokes. The whole school buzzed with excitement and anticipation.

The four friends had particular reason to be excited. Having heard them practising during their breaks, Fairy Godmother had asked them to close the show. Polly, Felicity and Daisy's stars nearly pinged off the ends of their wands when they heard. Only Holly remained icy cool.

"I'm not surprised," she said casually, when her friends asked her why she wasn't bouncing up and down with joy. "True talent will always be recognised."

Felicity had stayed up late every

night to make each
of them dresses for
their performance
and was very
pleased with
the result. She'd

found a pattern for an extra super
full skirt with a little matching top.
She'd made the straps out of tiny
gold stars stitched together.

Each of her fairy friends had
chosen their own colour of material.

As Felicity was making the dresses,
she got first choice and chose pink.
Daisy wanted green. Polly chose a
twinkly shade of yellow and Holly
checked the colour of the scenery
around the stage and thought a
deep red would help her stand out.

Felicity cut the pattern out of each
length of material. This was the
trickiest part. One wrong snip could
have them all wearing mini-skirts!

Every night Felicity's sewing machine had whirred. She had pinned and tacked and sewn hand stitches so tiny, she often lost her place. She embroidered tiny gold stars so the outfits looked as if they had been dusted with magic sparkle, and, as a special surprise, she sewed an extra large star right on the front of Holly's dress.

The fairies were thrilled when they saw their outfits.

"You're so good at sewing!" exclaimed Daisy.

"You're the *real* star of the show," said Polly, hugging her friend. "We're going to look magical on stage!"

Even Holly, still trying to remain cool (but whose tummy was doing somersaults inside), couldn't help giving a little skip when she saw the star on her dress.

* * *

With only half an hour until they
were due on stage for rehearsal,
Felicity was listening to Daisy recite
her poem. Daisy knew it off by heart,
but was so nervous she wanted to
go over it again and again.

"You know what would have been
really lovely?" said Felicity. "With a
name like Daisy and a poem about
flowers, I should have made you a
daisy costume with a skirt of petals."

Daisy agreed. "Oh, Felicity, what
a lovely idea, that would have been
perfect. What a shame we didn't
think of it earlier!"

Felicity looked at her watch. Less
than half-an-hour before they were
due on stage for rehearsal. Super
seamstress Felicity still had time to
make Daisy blossom!

Daisy wasn't so sure. Was there

really enough time? But Felicity was already rushing around like a fairy possessed. She found some scissors, a net curtain, glue and some yellow ribbon, and got to work. A hundred beautiful petals fell from the curtain as she snipped, and then, as there wasn't time to sew, she glued them all, one by one, layer upon layer, to the ribbon, so they hung down in gentle, transparent layers. It looked magical!

"Take off your skirt, turn around and close your eyes," Felicity said to Daisy, who was still reciting her poem under her breath.

Daisy undid her skirt and Felicity tied the petal-laden ribbon around Daisy's waist. It looked lovely. "There!" she said. "Open your eyes. A daisy for Daisy! You can wear this for your poem, and then pop your dress on over the top for our song." Daisy was speechless.

Just at that moment, Daisy's name was called. With shaky wings she made her way to the centre of the stage. If she were this wobbly for the rehearsal, what would she be like for the real thing?

The lights were bright and extremely hot. Just as Daisy took an extra deep breath to begin her poem, a fairy from the side signalled for her to stop – there was a problem with one of the lights. She stood patiently and waited for the wave to carry on. Just when she thought her little wings couldn't stand the heat any longer she was given the sign to continue.

Daisy began her poem beautifully. She was concentrating so hard, she didn't feel the petals on her skirt falling off one by one.

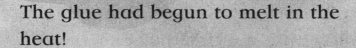

The glue had begun to melt in the heat!

The petals were so light that when they fell to reveal her little green tights, they didn't make a sound. It was only at the end when Daisy tried to find the corners of her skirt to curtsey, that she realised she had no skirt left to curtsey with!

Daisy wanted to hide forever with embarrassment.

"It was a disaster," she sighed.

"At least you were wearing your tights!" said Felicity, who felt a little responsible. "Everyone loved your outfit. I'll hand sew it for the real performance."

It was time for the four friends to rehearse their song. Polly had written the words to go along with 'Twinkle Twinkle Little Star' and the original idea had been that all four of them would start on stage, with Holly stepping forward to sing her solo in the spotlight before they all

joined in for the final verse. Holly
wanted to make more of an entrance
though, and decided not to appear
on stage until the point of her solo.

The rehearsal of the song was
uneventful and they all went home
humming, "Fairies of the world
unite…"

Felicity was still humming as she
worked late into the night, sewing
each petal on to Daisy's skirt by hand,
so that she wouldn't droop tomorrow.

* * *

The day of the concert. The fairies
had made a make-shift dressing room
in one of the classrooms and had
propped up mirrors on the desks.
Everyone had sent each other 'Good
Luck' cards, although Holly had
written 'Break a Leg' on hers, which
the others thought
strange.

"It's what theatre people do!" said Holly excitedly.

Fairy Godmother was sitting in the front row, together with other grand-looking fairies with wings larger than any of them had ever seen.

"There are so many fairies out there!" whispered Felicity, peeping out from behind the curtain.

"Don't tell me!" said Polly, her wings more of a flutter now than they had ever been.

* * *

The other fairies did their pieces with sparkle, smiles and small mishaps, but always to great applause.

It was almost time for their performance! They'd all been so nervous watching from the wings it was some time before Felicity noticed that Holly was missing. She looked around and asked some of the others, but none of them had seen Holly.

Daisy was about to go on. It would soon be time for them all to perform.

"You go on," Felicity said to Daisy. "I'll go and look for Holly."

"Don't be long, will you?" Polly said nervously.

* * *

Felicity found Holly sitting in front of the mirror in the classroom, a huge towel wrapped around her head.

"Holly! Thank goodness! Didn't you realise it's almost time for us to go on stage?"

Holly remained seated, staring into the mirror.

"I can't go on, I can't go on!" she wailed.

Felicity was shocked. Holly had seemed the calmest of them all – and here she was suffering from stage-fright!

"My career, it's over, OVER!" she continued, throwing her hands in the air.

Felicity crouched at her friend's feet and patted her knee.

"Holly, you'll be fine," she said gently. "You know you were born to perform."

"No!" moaned Holly. "I mean, I really *can't* go on stage. Look!" Holly whipped the towel off her head and there, stuck in her hair at a right angle to her head, was her hairbrush.

Holly cried tears of frustration. "I tried to give my hair an extra big curl at the end and I twirled the brush too tightly," she said miserably. "It's stuck!"

Felicity tried to pull the brush out but Holly screamed "YEOWW!" so loudly she thought the audience was sure to have heard her. When Felicity suggested they cut the brush out of Holly's hair she shouted even louder: "NO!"

Faintly, in the background, Felicity could hear Daisy announce the title of her poem, 'The Magic of Flowers'. There was no time to lose.

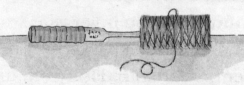

Strand by strand, Felicity carefully teased out Holly's hair from the brush, whilst Holly, now lost in desperate thoughts of a life without fame, covered her eyes.

Daisy was coming to the end of her poem. Polly put her head round the door in a panic.

"The show must go on!" said Felicity to her startled friend. "Just start without me."

Strand after strand she pulled, ordering Holly to keep her head straight and ignoring her yelps of pain. If she worked quickly there might just be time for Holly to make her solo.

The final piece of hair fell free and the fairies rushed to the wings just in time to hear Polly and Daisy finishing their verse.

"It's time for your big moment, your solo, Holly - go for it!" whispered Felicity, pushing her friend out on to the stage. But as she did so, Holly grabbed Felicity's hand and pulled her on to the stage behind her. The two friends stood together, holding hands in the spotlight, and sang. Then all four

of them linked hands for the final
verse. The audience went wild and
there were cries of "More, more!"
so the friends sang the last verse
again, this time with the
audience joining in.

Taking their curtseys, they skipped off the stage and into the wings, where they all hugged each other so hard their crowns popped off.

"I'm so sorry you didn't get a solo," said Felicity to Holly. "I know how important it was to you."

Holly was beaming. "Without you, Felicity, I would have missed my solo altogether! A duet with a best friend is just as good. In fact," she paused, "much better."

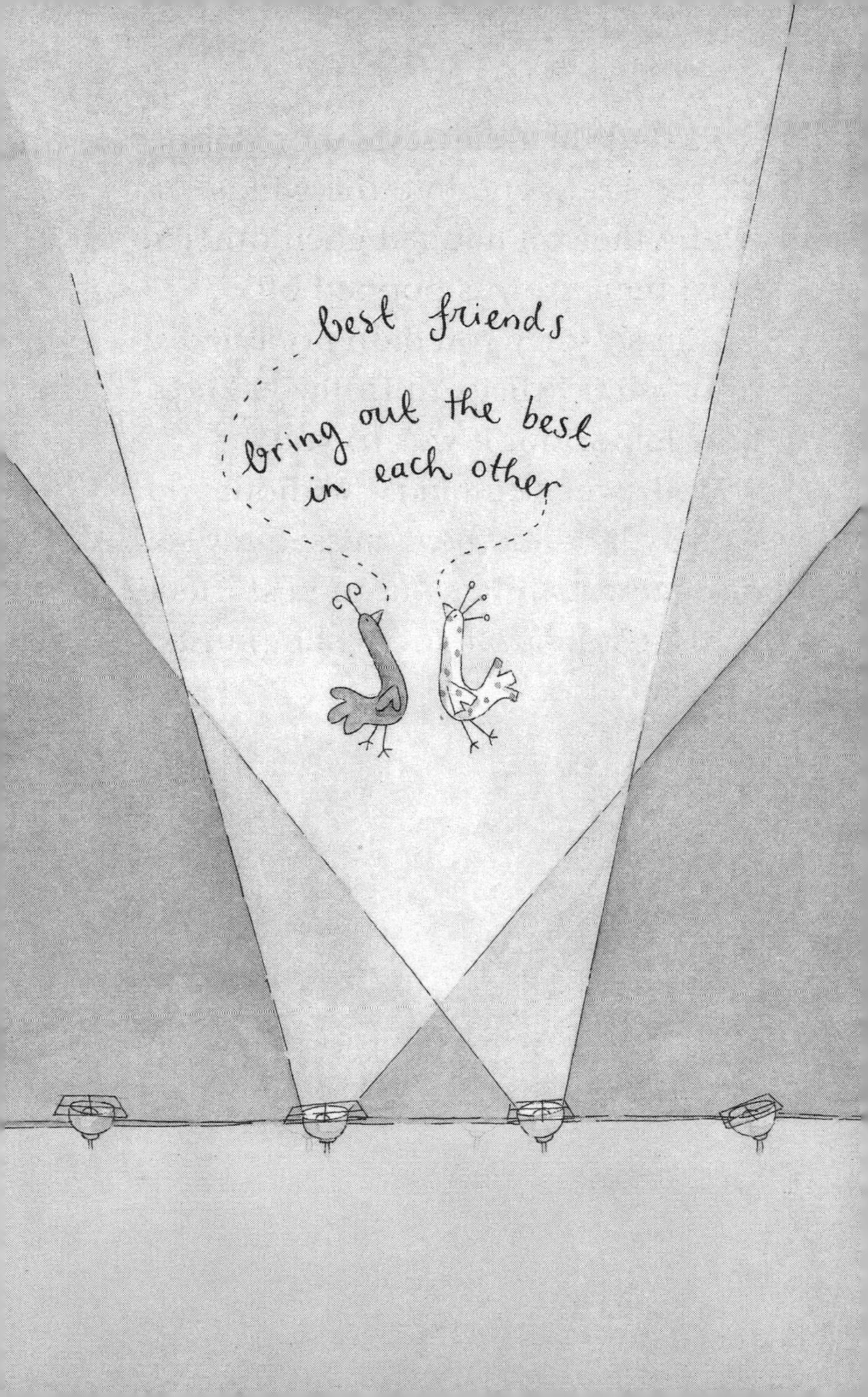
best friends
bring out the best
in each other

Dancing Dreams

It was Friday evening, and a trip to
the ballet had been arranged for the
students of Madame Plié's Dancing

School to see a performance of *Swan
Lake*. Everyone was very excited –
no one more so than Felicity Wishes.
Everything about going to the ballet
made her tingle with excitement:
the sound of the orchestra tuning
up, the muffled chatter of the crowd
waiting for the performance to
begin, the seats with their plump
red velvet cushions, the gold cherubs
with their beautiful, feathery wings
painted on the ceiling, but most of
all, the thought of what lay behind
the huge velvet curtain.

Holly had dashed into the theatre
the moment Madame Plié had
handed over the tickets, and was
now lying across four seats keeping
them all for her friends. Felicity,
Daisy and Polly arrived and sank
into their seats. They all began to
read the programmes that Madame
Plié passed down the row.

Inside was a picture of the famous Prima Fairy Ballerina, Natasha Milletova, who delighted audiences all over the world with her exquisite dancing. It was said that she was the most talented ballerina in living memory, and that to see her perform was a once in a lifetime opportunity. Tickets for all the performances had been sold out for months, and fairies were still queuing outside the theatre in the hope that a seat would become available at the last moment.

The fairies opened their packets of sweets and the orchestra began to tune their instruments. A bell sounded. The performance was about to begin! A few latecomers dashed in, and Felicity and the others had to tuck their legs in under their skirts and hold their breath so they could get past. Daisy cringed as she saw the person next to her sit on the chocolate truffle she had accidentally dropped. Holly nudged her and giggled. Then the lights dimmed, the orchestra started and the curtain went up with a tremendous swish...

From the first pirouette,
Felicity thought *Swan
Lake* was the most
wonderful ballet
she had ever
seen and Natasha
Milletova the most beautiful
ballerina imaginable.

Her wing control was
astounding. She could fly across the
stage effortlessly, her wings barely
appearing to move. She swooped
and dived and hovered and spun
with breathtaking grace and ease,
her tiny silver ballet shoes twinkling
magically under
the lights. No
wonder it was
rumoured that she
dipped her feet in
a tray of magic
dust before a
performance.

Felicity wanted the evening to go on forever!

When the curtain finally came down at the end of the performance, the audience rose to their feet and clapped and cheered. Even Madame Plié forgot to look stern and smiled broadly and clapped enthusiastically. The curtain rose again and Natasha swept back on to the stage to even wilder cheers and applause. Felicity tried to whistle but Madame gave her a stern look, so she stood on tiptoe and waved as hard as she could. Natasha received so many huge bouquets of flowers she could hardly carry them all, and people were throwing so many flowers from the audience it looked as if she was standing on a carpet of blooms. Felicity was sure that Natasha had given her a special smile.

After many encores the curtain finally came down and the lights went up.

The magic had ended.

The young fairies trooped out into the street, pointing their toes and fluttering their wings to the music still in their heads. It had been the best trip to the ballet Felicity could ever remember.

* * *

On Saturday morning, the fairies gathered at the dancing school. Most of them were still chattering about *Swan Lake*, but Felicity was still dreaming about it. All she

could think about were the bright
lights, the applause and the sight of
Natasha Milletova in her tutu and
silver shoes giving her a special
smile. If only she could dance as
well as Natasha.

"Young fairies!" barked Madame
Plié, clapping her hands. "Everyone
to the middle of the room and
assume the first position. We will
start with some gentle exercises
moving through the positions."

Holly, Polly, Daisy and the other
fairies carefully followed Madame
Plié's instructions, but Felicity was

too busy dreaming about *Swan Lake*. Although she started in first position she was still in it when the others had moved on to fourth!

"Felicity," whispered Daisy, as her arms swung past Felicity's into fifth position. "Are you stuck? You haven't moved!"

Madame Plié, who hadn't noticed Felicity, heard Daisy and snapped her fingers.

"I won't have talking in my class," she said to Daisy, who blushed the colour of a red rose.

Then Madame saw Felicity, who was standing with her feet in first position and her arms in third.

"Is there a reason why you aren't keeping up, Felicity?" asked Madame.

Felicity didn't hear her. In her head she was Natasha Milletova in the final scenes of *Swan Lake*.

Daisy nudged Felicity, who suddenly realised the entire class was staring at her.

"Sorry, Madame Plié," said Felicity. "I'll try to keep up."

"Please concentrate," said Madame, clearly irritated. "Concentration is extremely important in ballet. Perfect performances start with simple steps!"

Felicity didn't understand what Madame meant, but whatever Madame had said, Felicity's performance in class didn't get any better.

When they moved to the barre to practise their pliés, the long line of fairies rose and fell to the gentle tinkle of the music, all except Felicity, who managed to fall when everyone else had risen. In one exercise, Felicity still had her leg in front of her when the others moved theirs behind.

"I didn't mean to kick Daisy in the bottom!" she explained sheepishly, as the fairies untangled their legs from the mess her mistake had made.

Finally, the class came to an end. Tutus, tights and shoes were packed away and, giggling and chattering, the class began to empty. Felicity was still in her ballet clothes when Polly called over, "Are you coming to Sparkles for a hot chocolate with us, Felicity?"

"Er...yes," said Felicity vaguely.

There was always a scramble for chairs and tables at the café when class was over and the fairies didn't want to wait.

"We'll go on and get a table," said Polly, heading out of the door.

"Don't be long!" called Daisy, over her shoulder.

When her friends had gone, Felicity began to look at the pictures of famous Prima Fairy Ballerinas which were hanging on the wall. Each one looked poised and beautiful.

There was even a picture of a young Madame Plié, so-called because her pliés were so low her knees almost touched the floor. Felicity couldn't imagine Madame Plié being a young fairy, let alone being able to bend her knees very far.

Seeing photographs of the ballerinas brought back memories of the night before. The music came flooding back into her head.

She could smell the flowers, hear the

orchestra and see Natasha Milletova
come shimmering on to the stage.

Felicity began to dance, pretending
that she was Natasha, hearing the
audience gasp with delight as she
performed. Faster and faster she
danced, throwing herself around
the room.

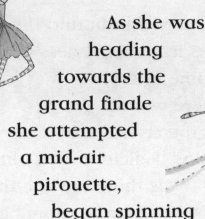

As she was
heading
towards the
grand finale
she attempted
a mid-air
pirouette,
began spinning
so fast she
became dizzy, lost
her bearings
and ricocheted
off the wall,
before landing
on the chandelier
hanging from the ceiling.
"Golly," thought
Felicity. "I think I got
a bit over-excited there."
But when she tried
to untangle herself from
the chandelier she found
she was stuck. Her wings

were wedged tight and the
ribbons from her shoes
had come undone
and were wound
round the crystal droplets.

"Hello?" Felicity called out.
"Is there anyone there?"
But the room below was
empty. All her friends had
left to go to Sparkles and
Madame Plié was nowhere
to be seen. What on earth was
Felicity going to do? She could
be here all night!

Every time she moved, the chandelier
tinkled prettily and made beautiful
rainbow patterns on the wall but, try
as she might, she couldn't wriggle
herself free.

"Help!" Felicity called at last. "Help!"
There was no answer.
The room was completely silent.

* * *

After what seemed like hours
(but was probably only a few
minutes), the door opened
and in walked a tiny figure
wearing woolly socks and a woolly
jumper over a pair of grey tights.

Felicity was about to shout "HELP!"
when she realised that the fairy below
her was none other than Natasha
Milletova.

Felicity couldn't believe it! Prima
Fairy Ballerina Milletova below her
in Madame Plié's Dancing School!
She couldn't possibly ask the world
famous ballerina to remove her from
a chandelier. It would be just TOO
embarrassing.

To Felicity's amazement, Natasha
walked to the centre of the room and
began to do the same exercises that
Madame Plié had been doing with
the class earlier that day. Where were
the amazing arabesques and perfect

pirouettes that Felicity and her friends
had seen on stage?

First position, second position, third
position, fourth and fifth. Several
times she went through this routine,
watching herself in the mirrors around
the room.

Felicity could feel her nose
beginning to twitch. The chandelier
was very dusty.

"Oh no!" thought Felicity in a panic,
"I'm going to sneeze!"

"ATISHOO!" Felicity sneezed so hard
the chandelier tinkled like a
thousand raindrops falling.

Natasha looked up sharply
at the young fairy hanging
helplessly from the light.

"I'm so sorry," Felicity
shouted down. "I'm stuck!"

Natasha flew up to Felicity
and quickly untangled her wings
and unwound the ribbons from

her shoes. Felicity felt a bit dizzy from hanging upside down, so Natasha held her hand as they flew back down.

"Are you alright?" enquired the Prima Ballerina, finding Felicity a chair to sit on. "How on earth did you start a ballet class and end up tangled in a chandelier?"

Felicity blushed. How could she tell Natasha that after seeing *Swan Lake* she had been daydreaming in her ballet class about being her, and had got carried away? It was so embarrassing. This was Natasha Milletova!

But Felicity was feeling too dizzy to think of a tale tall enough to save her blushes, so she bit her lip and told the truth.

"I couldn't believe it when you came in," said Felicity shyly. "I *thought* it was you, but then when I saw you do the same exercises we do in class I thought it couldn't possibly be."

Natasha smiled at Felicity, who was glowing with rosy cheeks.

"All dancers, whatever level, must start with exercises," said Natasha. "It warms up our muscles so we don't get injured."

"But what about the flying arabesques?" asked Felicity. "What about the fun stuff?"

Natasha began to laugh. "The fun stuff is actually very hard work. You know all the movements you see on stage?"

Felicity nodded enthusiastically.

"Each one of those has its beginnings in the exercises you do as a young fairy. The more experienced you get, the more you put the exercises together to make something magical."

So *that* was what Madame Plié had been meaning when she'd said, "Perfect performances start with simple steps."

"But what are you doing here?" asked Felicity. Even with her woolly tights and jumper Natasha still seemed impossibly glamorous.

"I'm dancing in *The Nutcracker* this evening," said Natasha. "I wanted to get away from the theatre and go through some steps in peace and quiet. Madame said I could use the room after your class had finished. I didn't expect to have an audience!"

"I'm sorry," said Felicity. "I'll leave you alone. Thank you so much for helping me."

"I don't know your name," said Natasha, as Felicity headed for the door.

"Felicity," said Felicity quietly. "Felicity Wishes."

Natasha reached into her bag and, after some searching, pulled out a pair of tiny, silver ballet shoes, which she handed to Felicity. Felicity's mouth fell open as she recognised them.

"Are they really the ones you wore last night?" she asked.

"Yes," said Natasha, already heading back to the barre. "Now off you go, so I can practise. I'm sure I'll see you again soon."

Felicity didn't hear her, she was so busy saying thank you. Then she flew as fast as she could to Sparkles. What a wonderful gift! What a once in a lifetime meeting. The others were never going to believe it!

When Felicity finally got to the café she showed her friends the tiny silver shoes.

"There's something tucked inside," said Holly, peering at them closely.

Felicity reached in and pulled out four tickets for that evening's performance of *The Nutcracker*. It was only then that she remembered Natasha's parting words. She really *would* be seeing her again soon!

the most magical
surprises

always turn up in
the most unexpected
places !

COMING SOON

* * ✶ * *

Four more Felicity Wishes
story collections:

* * ✶ * *

Clutter Clean Out

Designer Drama

Newspaper Nerves

Star Surprise

* * ✶ * *

Also available in the Felicity Wishes range:

Felicity Wishes: Snowflakes and Sparkledust

It is time for spring to arrive in Little Blossoming but there is
a problem and winter is staying put. Can Felicity Wishes get
the seasons back on track?

Felicity Wishes: Secrets and Surprises

Felicity Wishes is planning her birthday party but it seems none of her friends can come. Will Felicity end up celebrating her birthday alone?

Felicity Wishes: Friendship and Fairyschool

It's nearly time for Felicity Wishes to leave fairyschool, but she has no idea what kind of fairy she wants to be. Will Felicity find her true talent?

Felicity Wishes has lots to say in these fantastic little books:

Little Book of Friendship

Little Book of Birthdays

Little Book of Wishes

Little Book of Happiness

Little Book of Love

Little Book of Peace

Little Book of Hiccups

Little Book of Every Day Wishes

Little Book of Fun